The Spy In Black

By Joseph Storer Clouston

Limited Edition no:

0235

Text from the 1917 edition published by Wm Blackwood & Sons, Edinburgh & London
Published by Seabridge in association with AOP (Another Orkney Production)
Mill House, Willow Road, Kirkwall, Orkney KW15 1NJ
Book design and artwork: Peter Needham.
Dust jacket design: Pat Sutherland.
Printed by Ambassador Litho.
All materials copyright AOP 2007
Text of THE SPY IN BLACK copyright the estate of J Storer Clouston.
Copyright of additional chapters rest with the individual authors.
Photographs copyright Orkney Library and Archive. Reproduced by kind permission.
The publishers gratefully acknowledge the financial assistance given by
The Department of Nordic Studies, Orkney College and Orkney Islands Council.
All rights reserved.
The contents of this book may not be reproduced in any form without written permission from AOP.

ISBN 978-0-9553667-1-0

ACKNOWLEDGEMENTS

There are many people without whose help and advice this book would not have been possible. For any whose names should have been listed below and are not, please forgive this oversight.

Firstly our thanks to the Clouston family who allowed this new edition to go ahead and in particular Jane for her thoughts, comments and a wonderful forward, and Ingirid for her energy and help in identifying the route taken by Lieutenant Belke on his motorcycle journey across Orkney.

Geoffrey Stell, Donna Heddle and Sarah Jane Gibbon not only wrote essays but offered support and suggestions. Geoffrey must bear some responsibility for the idea of publishing this new edition.

The Orkney Rangers Sandra Miller and Elaine Clarke always provided good ideas liberally sprinkled with their usual humour.

It would not be fair to discuss the search for the route without mentioning the late Daphne Lorimer who had already gone out into the hills to locate it and whose death robbed us of her findings.

Peter Needham has guided the book's progress from the initial idea to the printed word. Any errors are not of his making.

Janice Edwards, as well as checking the text, gave helpful advice and information at all hours of the day.

One of the most outstanding and perhaps not acknowledged enough resources in Orkney is the Orkney Archive and Library. We are indebted to Alison Fraser, David Mackie and all of the staff there, for without their help this work could never have happened.

Ola Gorie offered helpful advice, information and an interesting perspective as one of the few Orcadian extras in the film with a speaking part!

Many others offered their wisdom including:

Ronnie Johnson, Margaret Clouston and the Orphir WRI, Bryony Dixon, Barbara Foulkes, Hilda Firth, Sandy Firth, Dave Gray, Elaine Grieve, Sheena Leith, John McDonald, Rose Seagrief, Bruce Sutherland, Angela Taylor, Graham Worrall, Sonja, John and Martin Wishart and not forgetting the much missed Day Wishart.

AOP (ANOTHER ORKNEY PRODUCTION)

AOP (Another Orkney Production) is a voluntary organisation that specialises in heritage and arts projects with Orkney as the common theme.

The publication of this book is as a direct result of REFLECTING SCAPA FLOW, a four part project which received funding from, amongst others, The Heritage Lottery Fund, Scottish Natural Heritage and Orkney Heritage Society.

CONTENTS

FOREWORD

BY JANE K. CLOUSTON

JSC, or to be more formal, my grandfather, Joseph Storer Clouston, was actually an unknown factor in our family. Only our father ever knew him. The rest was hearsay.

He was apparently an acknowledged scholar and, judging by what I have recently read of his novels, a competent and entertaining journeyman writer of books which were not pretentious. As a naturalised German it is an interesting convolution having me write a foreword to such a novel but I love a good spy yarn and will forgive him his everyman presentation of a German.

As the sins of the fathers are visited upon their children and their children's children I assume that he was bossy (the servants loved him but took care to avoid him on his off-days), did not always know what he wanted, someone else caused his bad moods and allowed him to be bad tempered, chaos reigned in his study and he put off writing assignments till the very last moment, library books (even from such illustrious libraries as the State Library in Salzburg) changed owners (we are of Viking descent)!

He was open for new ideas, was always an interested listener and person to talk to. I deducted his admiration for George Bernhard Shaw as I later discovered that quotes ascribed to JSC were actually from GBS! Jo showed good taste in his choice of hero!

Jane K. Clouston
Erding, 05.03.2007

INTRODUCTION

Why a new edition of *The Spy In Black?*

The Spy In Black was first published in 1917 by Blackwood and Son of Edinburgh and is the best known of the many novels written by J Storer Clouston. It is surprising that, although well known, the book has been out of print since the 1940s and has been therefore not readily available to present day readers.

There can be no doubt that Clouston is an important Orcadian writer. A simple glance at his bibliography shows the extent of his work both as an historian and a novelist.

He also served his local community over many years as a county councillor and then convenor. A quick look through council reports in archive editions of the Orcadian and the Orkney Herald will find his name turning up regularly.

One of the reasons that *The Spy In Black* has remained a familiar name is due to the 1939 film version of the story by director Michael Powell and screenplay writer Emeric Pressburger. This was their first collaboration, before they went on to make such classics as *A Matter of Life and Death.*

The film starred the renowned German actor Conrad Veidt and British actress Valerie Hobson and has become part of modern Orkney folklore through the stories of the host of Orcadian extras, not to mention the first successful walk up the cliff behind the Old Man of Hoy complete with motorcycle (perhaps due to German ingenuity?), and the stone circle at the cliff top.

An intriguing fact is that *The Spy In Black* was not the first of Clouston's stories to be made into a film, in fact it was the last.

In 1917, the very year that *The Spy In Black* was published, the film *The Mystery Of No.47* was directed by Otis Thayer. Two versions were made of *The Lunatic At Large.* The first in 1921 was directed by and starred Henry Edwards and the second, released in 1927, was directed by Fred Newmeyer and starred Leon Errol and Dorothy Mackaill.

In 1937 French director Marcel Carne made *Drole et Drame ou L'Etrange Aventure de Docteur Molyneux.* The English title *Laughter and Drama or The Strange Adventure of Dr Molyneux* is a direct translation from the French whilst the Americans called it *Bizarre Bizarre.* Clouston's original story was called *His First Offence.*

There is little doubt that the title familiar to most Orcadians is *The Spy In Black.* 90 years on seems a good time to make it available again!

Moya McDonald
AOP (Another Orkney Production)

JOSEPH STORER CLOUSTON – THE HISTORIAN

Dr Sarah Jane Gibbon

JOSEPH STORER CLOUSTON was born in Cumberland on the 23rd May 1870. He was one of three children born of Thomas Clouston M.D. and Harriet Storer. Thomas was a highly renowned mental expert, and a devotee of Orkney where he was born and where he spent the summers with his family. Thus Storer was in Orkney each summer and he grew to love the place immensely. Orkney was his spiritual home, and he was very proud of his Orcadian ancestry.

Clouston trained in law at Oxford but he never practised, choosing instead to become a writer. He lived most of his life in Edinburgh, although each summer was spent in Orkney. He made Smoogro House in Orphir his permanent residence where he lived for some thirty years, until his death in 1944. He was Convenor of the county council from 1930, and chairman of the Orkney Harbours Commission from 1935. He was a successful fiction writer and transferred his ability to write a good story to his historical writings, which made them more desirable.

Clouston was one of several prominent scholars investigating the history of Orkney at the turn of the twentieth century. Among the most influential men, in terms of their contributions to Orkney's historical record, were Alfred Wintle Johnston (founder of the Viking Society) and Hugh Marwick (the expert on Orkney place-names). Clouston knew, and corresponded with, both gentlemen as well as writing to several prominent Nordic scholars, such as Bull, Jakobsen, Østberg, Roussell, Shetelig, and Taranger. At this time, there was a surge of scholarly interest in the Norse History of Orkney. This interest was rooted in Romantic, nationalistic ideas that were permeating throughout Western Europe at the time. In Orkney, followers of these ideas, through their scholarly research, perpetuated the Viking "Golden Age": a concept that is still upheld today. Clouston, Marwick and Johnston, as a result of their research, presented medieval Orkney as an affluent, semi-autonomous power. They believed Scandinavian culture and institutions were the basis of Orkney's medieval past and therefore, their histories were dominated by Scandinavian comparisons. They "Scandinavianised" Orkney in an attempt to glorify it and separate it from the rest of Scotland. All three historians seemed to lament the "Scottification" of Orkney in the later medieval period, and no-one more so than Clouston.

But Clouston's motivation was not only to serve Romantic – nationalistic ideas; he had a genuine curiosity in Orkney's past. His History of Orkney, the culmination of many years of research, tells, in a strong and colourful narrative, the history of Orkney from prehistoric times to the demise of the Stewart Earls in the sixteenth century. Yet, this History of Orkney is much more than an historical narrative. Within its pages the reader can learn about many of the intricacies of medieval Orkney, of institutions, of houses and field systems, the church and the government of the islands. What the reader will not find is a socio-economic analysis of the past. Clouston's interest was in politics, religion and people and these are the subjects that occupied his research. More than anything else, it is his interest in the people of the past that makes him stand out as amongst his peers.

Storer Clouston was more than an historian; he was an antiquarian in all its positive nuances. He collected and transcribed many legal documents (some published in Records of the Earldom of Orkney, 1914). He also, very importantly, visited local people and talked to them about their homes, their families and their histories. He gathered a wealth of information, preserved neatly in his notebooks, which otherwise would have been lost.

Clouston also tried his hand at excavation, and, for his time, he was reasonably methodical. Again, without his investigations we would not know of the medieval remains at the Bu of Cairston in Stromness, The Wirk in Rousay or Tammaskirk in Rendall. Clouston's daughter Marjory recollected her father deciphering documents, and digging in "bitterly cold weather". She warmly recalled that "his enthusiasm was infectious and his curiosity about Orkney's past and his affection for her every mood and colour were absolutely limitless".

This is why his historical research is so important; he was passionate about Orkney, and passionate about discovering all he could about its past inhabitants. Clouston focused on the individual and, as a result, produced excellent work that was less obsessed with the trappings of institutionalisation than his contemporaries. His interest in people and in the Norse period, meant of course, that he was intrigued by the sagas, and in particular the character Sweyn Asliefson, of whom he seems to have been particularly fond. His interest in the sagas and his desire for Nordic influences on the past can be seen in much of his academic work.

Other scholars, including myself, have, over the years, criticised Clouston for his over-zealous Scandinavianising of the past, and this is a problem. But it is by no means insurmountable. His sometimes over-Scandinavianised interpretations, when considered in their context, do not detract from his scholarship. Through his meticulous collection of old documents, charters and deeds Clouston gained an incomparable knowledge of Orkney's legal system that provided him with a basic understanding of society in Orkney beyond any of his contemporaries.

His wide-ranging studies were derived from his knowledge of a variety of sources. For example, the documentary sources he gathered led to his research into runrig farming, townships, houses, mills and taxation; his interest in the Orkneyinga Saga, inspired his research into Norse Castles, goodmen and hirdmen, muster stations, beacon sites, Bu estates and the Orkney Lawthing; his curiosity of genealogy and finding the oldest Orcadian families produced studies of Odal families, old Orkney names and of heraldry. The list is almost endless.

Clouston lived and breathed Orkney's history and his contributions to historical research should not be underestimated. His ability as a scholar is attested by the endurance of his published works, which are still read by students of Orkney's past. Clouston laid many of the foundation stones of medieval studies in Orkney and for that he should be properly acknowledged. Clouston was a man of learning, knowledge, detail, ability and passion, and all of these things are combined within the pages of his historical writings. His meticulous and heart-felt studies are an inspiration and thoroughly deserve their place amongst the greatest contributions to our knowledge of Orkney's past.

Dr Sarah Jane Gibbon is a Lecturer in the Department of Cultural Studies at Orkney College. She completed a joint honours degree in history and archaeology at Glasgow University where she did a research masters in archaeology, her subject being "Norse Castles in Orkney." Whilst working at the Orkney Archive she began studying for her PhD with the UHI Millennium Institute at Orkney College. She completed her thesis with the added distinction of being the first person to complete a PhD in the short history of Orkney College. Her subject was to look into the formation of the medieval parochial system in Orkney by means of a landscape approach.

CLOUSTON – THE WRITER OF FICTION

Dr Donna Heddle

JOSEPH STORER CLOUSTON had a keen interest in the Orkney Islands, where he also made his home for most of his life. He was a prolific writer. His books include *Vandrad the Viking, The Adventures of M. D'Haricot, Colonel Bunker, The Prodigal Father, Tales of King Fido, Carrington's Cases,* and *Beastmark the Spy.* One of his most successful works was the thriller *The Lunatic at Large,* which yielded several sequels, owing to the demand from the public.

His writings included texts on the history of Orkney and also some fiction set there, most notably *The Spy in Black,* the best known of his many espionage tales and thrillers. The story about German agents plotting against the British fleet anchored at the Orkney islands captured the imagination of readers on both sides of the Atlantic and was originally published as a serialised thriller in the New York Tribune Sunday review in 1918. It is a prime example of the genre of British fiction known as invasion literature. The genre was extremely influential in England in shaping politics, national policies and popular perceptions in the years leading up to the First World War, and still remains a part of popular culture in the form of science fiction.

Invasion literature flourished most vigorously between 1871 and the outbreak of World War I in 1914. The genesis of the genre was in 1871 with the publication of the short story *The Battle of Dorking* by George Tomkyns Chesney[1], which was a fictional account of a German invasion of Britain. *The Battle of Dorking* enjoyed wide success and created a huge appetite for stories about hypothetical invasions by foreign powers. It reached its zenith by 1914 – the genre had amassed a

corpus of over 400 books, many best-sellers, and a world-wide audience – as well as its critics who considered that it exacerbated the already volatile relationship between Britain, France, and Germany.

Rumours of planned German invasion rose to fever pitch by 1906. Claims about the scale of German invasion preparations grew increasingly ambitious. The number of German spies was put at between 60,000 and 300,000 – despite the total German community in Britain being no more than 44,000 people. Subsequent research has since shown that no significant German espionage network existed in Britain at this time.

The concerns raised in invasion literature were given as the official rationale for the creation of the Secret Service Bureau in 1909. The Bureau later become MI5 and MI6.

THE SPY IN BLACK

The film version of *The Spy in Black* has become far better known than Clouston's original novel; Powell and Pressburger's film has even exerted an influence on such relatively recent movies as Richard Marquand's *Eye of the Needle* (1981). The film is markedly different from the text and has a darker, more convoluted ending. Pressburger rewrote everything in the book except the Orkney Islands setting and some details of the basic plot. The resulting film, about a World War I German plot to sink the British fleet at anchor in the Orkney Islands, starring Conrad Veidt and Valerie Hobson, was considered to be so good that the British distributor, Alexander Korda, held it back from release for nearly a year until real events added to the film's topicality – the plot concerned a World War I German U-boat 29 and the attempt by its captain to sink the British fleet; in late 1939, a real-life German U-Boat, under the command of Captain Gunther Prien, sank a British battleship in Scapa Flow in the Orkney Islands. This was one of the first major naval actions of the war in European waters, and the event became the subject of headlines around the world. Columbia Pictures, the American distributor, retitled the movie *U-Boat 29* and it proved a great success on both sides of the Atlantic, tapping as it did into the zeitgeist of the era: fear of invasion allied to a belief in the superiority of the Allied forces.

NARRATIVE STRUCTURE

Lieutenant Von Belke is represented as the hero of the book – until the final twist when we discover the identity of the real "Spy in Black". We first meet him in media res – in the middle of the action of the text and it is his adventures that the reader follows in breathless anticipation until the final revelation of his duping by Commander Blacklock.

The story itself is told in five parts:

Part I: The Narrative of Lieutenant von Belke (of the German Navy)

Part II: A Few Chapters by the Editor

Part III: Lieutenant von Belke's Narrative Resumed

Part IV: Lieutenant von Belke's Narrative Concluded

Part V: A Few Concluding Chapters by the Editor

The rationale behind this elaborate narrative structure is to confuse and perplex the reader – just as von Belke will be confused and perplexed by the machinations of the Spy in Black. It is noticeable that von Belke, who starts off as the person who appears to know what the situation is, and is pursued by those

who suspect something is going on, becomes bewildered and confused – and those around him seem to have a better perception of events than himself. The reader gradually becomes detached from von Belke as he moves from what is essentially a very British hero telling his story of derring do directly to the reader to the quintessentially didactic Prussian described in the third person on p.301,

Von Belke looked at her for a moment with frowning brow and folded arms. Then all he said was –
"Germany's cause is sacred!"
Her eyes opened very wide.
"Then what is right for Germany is wrong for her enemies?"
"Naturally. How can Germany both be right – as she is, and yet be wrong?"
"I-I don't think you quite understand what I mean," she said with a puzzled look.
"Germany never will," said Blacklock quietly. "That is why we are at war."[2]

THE PLOT

The plot itself deals with the assemblage of the dramatis personae in the "Windy Isles" over a few days, and uses a series of startling coincidences and opportunities reminiscent of James Bond films, and of boys' adventure stories which were so close to the heart of Storer Clouston.

Lieutenant Von Belke of the German Navy U Boat division is landed secretly on an un-named Scottish island referred to as one of the "Windy Isles" – as the book was written during World War I and published in 1917 there were issues of state secrecy involved and it would have been unpatriotic to identify where the grand fleet lay at anchor, although in point of fact everybody knew that the fleet was in Scapa Flow and that Orkney was a reserved area, requiring a passport for access.

Von Belke finds himself on Orkney with a motorbike and most of the first narrative section deals with his attempts to dodge various pursuers during the next day until he can meet his contact on the second night and his vicissitudes after the breakdown of his motorbike. He sets boobytraps for pursuers and cuts a phone line so his existence cannot remain a secret for long – on a small exposed Orkney Island there are not many places to hide.

Meanwhile, Rev Alexander Burnett, minister of a parish in the south of Scotland, is sent a newspaper clipping about a minister who is about to retire from his post in the Windy Islands. After the Sunday service he meets a man from Lancashire, who suggests he applies for the vacant post in the Windy Islands. He decides to stay with a friend in Edinburgh called Drummond but receives a telegram purporting to be from Drummond saying that a friend will pick him up and drive him to Edinburgh. Strangely enough, Drummond's friend is the man from Lancashire, and his chauffeur, we are told, bears a striking resemblance to Mr Burnett, which Mr Burnett does not notice. Mr Burnett and the man from Lancashire are driven along the coast; a light is spotted, Mr Burnett gets out to investigate and is rendered insensible by the chauffeur.

Lieutenant Topham of the Royal Navy goes to see Drummond and tells him they've just fished Rev Burnett out of the sea. He had been hit on the head and tied up. Topham asks about the telegrams (Drummond was sent one to say Burnett wasn't coming and he was suspicious of that) and also mentions Commander Blacklock, an officer on special service. This is an important point for the reader to note – although we don't realise it until the end of the book when all is revealed.

"Mr Burnett" takes the ferry to Orkney. On the ferry he meets an attractive lady, Miss Holland, who has been engaged as governess by a family called Craigie – who provide a somewhat anachronous humorous subplot in their subsequent search for her. Miss Holland claims to know "Mr Burnett" and they spend a good deal of time in conversation. This is another "the reader is warned" moment.

Von Belke meets his contact at last. It is "Mr Burnett", who reveals himself to be Herr Adolph Tiel of the German Secret Service and that the man from Lancashire is in fact Schumann, the head of the German spy ring.

Von Belke is put into a back room in the cottage and greatly resents his treatment from Tiel whom he does not consider his social equal. He is later joined by a lady who purports to be "Miss Burnett" – she is introduced to von Belke as another member of the spy ring. She is in reality the governess, Miss Holland, and von Belke starts to take a romantic interest in her.

Von Belke is then introduced to Lt Ashington of the Royal Navy who appears to be ready to betray the fleet to the German U-Boat squadron. Von Belke, who is portrayed throughout as the soul of honour, is disgusted by Ashington. He notes:

I bowed to Captain Ashington – I could not bring myself to touch his hand, and we left his great gross figure sipping whisky-and -soda .
"What do you think of him?" asked Tiel.
"He seems extremely competent," I answered candidly.
"But what an unspeakable scoundrel!"[2]

Von Belke returns to his U-boat and arranges for a squadron of submarines to be ready to attack the fleet.

The final twist in the plot is really quite surprising – we find out that Tiel was really Commander Blacklock all along. It is Blacklock who is the eponymous Spy in Black. The British Secret Service had found Mr Burnett and worked out what was going on. Blacklock had replaced Tiel and had met Miss Holland on the ferry. She had joined them at the cottage pretending to be another German spy pretending to be the sister of the Mr Burnett. It was all a plot to destroy the submarine squadron with Ashington as the so-called traitor. Von Belke was nothing more than their dupe and is arrested.

Blacklock, having respect for von Belke's honour, seeks to save him from being shot. The German is furious and disgusted with Miss Holland, whom he now perceives as having been a decoy to distract his attention. He is led away fuming and the reader is left with a rather unlikely romantic happy ending in which Commander Blacklock, stirred by the plucky British spirit of Miss Holland, declares his love, which is reciprocated, and the book closes on their first kiss.

CONCLUSION

The Spy in Black is quite a straightforward romantic adventure story in many ways but there are points of interest – the clever narrative structure discussed above is one and the depiction of von Belke as a man of honour and almost as a British hero in many respects up until the reader's alienation from him at the end of the book is another. This concept of the noble enemy who is in some capacity like ourselves, and that class, not nationality, is the unifying factor is not new but Storer

Clouston ably exhibits this in his depiction of von Belke and his relationship of mutual understanding and respect with the man who is his enemy – Commander Blacklock.

Storer Clouston does not omit to wave the flag, however, and the reader is left in no doubt that the British are on the side of might and right. He also waves the flag for Orkney by depicting the islanders as intelligent and well informed – the servant who looks after von Belke at the cottage is in the plot against him as well.

Storer Clouston gives the last word in the novel to an Orcadian, who says of Blacklock

"Of course I knew fine what he was after," said she. (3)

This is more perhaps than the reader did!

Dr Donna Heddle has been programme leader for the BA (Hons) Culture Studies of the Highlands and Islands since June 1999 and is based at Orkney College as Head of the Department of Cultural Studies. She was previously employed by the Dept of English Literature and the Centre for Continuing Education at the University of Edinburgh. She has been involved in a number of NPP cultural projects involving technology and education. A book entitled Northern Heritage has just been published as a result of these projects. A new UHI research centre in interdisciplinary Northern and Nordic studies is being developed by Donna at Orkney and Shetland Colleges. She will also be developing a new postgraduate MA in Highlands and Islands Literature.

NOTES

1. *George Tomkyns Chesney, "The Battle of Dorking", Blackwood's Magazine, Edinburgh, 1871. Blackwood's was a highly respected magazine with a wide readership, including political figures.*

2. *The Spy In Black, Storer Clouston's Omnibus, Joseph Storer Clouston, William Blackwood and Sons Ltd, Edinburgh and London, 1948, p.237*

3. *ibid., p.307. The remark is actually made in respect of Blacklock's love for Miss Holland but serves as a useful coda for the book.*

1917 – THE STATE OF THE WORLD

THE VIEW FROM THE AUTHOR'S WINDOW:
SMOOGRO HOUSE AND SCAPA FLOW IN 1917 AND 1939

Geoffrey Stell

OUTSTANDING SEA VIEWS south across Scapa Flow is how the setting of seven-bedroomed Smoogro House at Orphir was recently and successfully advertised for sale by an Orkney estate agent. Unusually, given the hyperbole that is customary in property literature, this was a perfectly accurate, un-exaggerated description of the location of Smoogro. Associated with one of the few copses of trees on the Orkney Mainland, the former residence of Storer Clouston, author of The Spy in Black, stands on gently sloping ground above Swanbister Bay, commanding a truly enviable prospect of the extensive waters of Scapa Flow with a distant southern horizon framed by the islands of Hoy, Flotta, Burray and South Ronaldsay. Smoogro also gains a physical advantage from the fact that it rises through three storeys, a feature which betrays its origins as a 17th-century tower house, later added to and altered in the early 19th and early 20th centuries.

As viewed from Smoogro House in 1917, Scapa Flow presented a busy, bustling scene quite different from today's relatively placid panorama. The wartime station of the Grand Fleet since before hostilities began in August 1914, the Flow was being regularly used by over 120 warships and numberless auxiliary craft, their crowded ranks gradually swollen by the arrival of American troopships and warships following the entry of the United States of America into the conflict on 6 April 1917. The principal fleet anchorage lay to the north of Flotta, clearly in view of Smoogro. In the immediate foreground, Swanbister Bay was used by seaplanes whose main business was to conduct reconnaissance patrols in search of German U-boats. On the western

shore of the bay below Toy Ness, there was a landing strip, little more than a field, which served as a naval airfield and which was about to be developed as an improved replacement for the main seaplane base at Houton. Not completed until well after the Armistice in 1918, the base incorporated a jetty which originally comprised timber linking sections and still remains one of the most conspicuous surviving relics of World War I along the north coast of the Flow.

This unassuming coastal site, known to the Royal Navy as Smoogro, is redolent with history. In the summer of 1917 it was to this landing strip that pilots first began experimental flights from the deck of HMS Furious, a battlecruiser which had been converted into a proto-aircraft carrier with a flying-off deck in place of her forward gun. The experiments were carried a stage further on 2 August when Commander Edward Dunning successfully flew his Sopwith Pup aircraft from Smoogro onto the flying-off deck of Furious whilst it was sailing across the Flow at about 26 knots into a headwind, the first-ever aircraft to land on a moving ship. A repeat experiment five days later ended in tragedy when the aircraft went over the side and Dunning was killed. Success and failure together, however, were events of huge, world-wide significance in the development of naval aviation and in the creation of aircraft carriers with landing-on, as well as flying-off, decks.

Viewed from Smoogro the capital ships of the Grand Fleet at anchor must have always made an impressive sight, and were the subject of some fine paintings by war artists. But, as with warships of any age, overt pride in their mighty appearance was often tempered by a secret fear of their vulnerability. Their deployment was known to involve serious risk, as was eloquently pointed out by Winston Churchill, then First Sea Lord, when he famously remarked that Admiral Jellicoe is the only commander on either side capable of losing the war in a single afternoon.

It was from and back to Scapa Flow that the main battle fleet led by Admiral Jellicoe's flagship, HMS Iron Duke, sailed to engage with the German High Seas Fleet off Jutland in May and June of 1916. It was also from Scapa, in the immediate aftermath of the Battle of Jutland, that one of the warships engaged in that action, HMS Hampshire, set out on its ill-fated and never-to-be accomplished mission to take Lord Kitchener to Russia. The following year, 1917, witnessed a creeping but significant intensification of the U-boat menace, the prevailing sombre but determined mood lifted by loyal celebrations on the occasion of a rainswept royal visit by King George V in June. The scene was rudely shattered – literally – by the blowing up at anchor off Flotta of HMS Vanguard on 9 July 1917. With the loss of over 1,000 men, the destruction of this 19,560-ton battleship has remained the greatest single human disaster ever to have afflicted Scapa Flow. Vanguard was completely blown apart amidships, evidently, like the Bulwark (1914) and Natal (1915), the result of an internal explosion caused by stored cordite which had become unstable.

Faulty ammunition was the formal verdict of the official inquiry but, then as now, a dramatic event of this nature inevitably triggered fears of sabotage, terrorism and espionage. After three years of all-out war, military and civilian spies were thought to be everywhere. Indeed, espionage was real and had become rife. Margaretha Geertruide Zelle, a Dutch dancer known to history as Mata Hari, had spent these war years in Paris in the employment of the German secret service, betraying to them the military secrets of the Allied officers with whom she shared intimate relations.

1917 was the year in which she was identified as a spy and in which she was convicted and judicially executed by the French. 1917 was also the year in which the United States of America, unique among the great powers in not possessing civilian espionage systems and military intelligence units, passed an Espionage Act on 15 June, just two months after its entry into the conflict. President Woodrow Wilson clearly saw such an enactment as one of the major priorities of a newly combatant nation-in-arms.

The years immediately preceding the outbreak of World War II in 1939 witnessed a significant burgeoning of espionage networks, particularly those associated with the assertive, military-minded régimes in Germany and Japan. It was a period of heightened apprehension and dark foreboding throughout much of the world, especially Europe. The creation of the film version of The Spy in Black and its first release in July 1939 thus fed an appetite for an ever-popular genre at a time when the public at large was more receptive than usual to the heady fascination and fear engendered by spy stories. It is interesting to note in parenthesis that an acute awareness of the dangers of duplicity returned again in the Cold War years when the stakes were even higher, a mood that was well captured and reflected in a cult of spymaster novels such as those by Ian Fleming and John le Carré.

Only loosely based on the novel from which it takes its name, the highly acclaimed film of The Spy in Black by Michael Powell and Emeric Pressburger takes considerable liberties with the original characterisation and plot to create a story of much greater mobility and complexity. Clouston himself was reportedly not best pleased by these changes but they were clearly appreciated by contemporary cinema audiences who had acquired a taste for action-packed spy films such as Alfred

Hitchcock's classic 1935 adaptation of John Buchan's Scottish-based novel of 1915, The Thirty-Nine Steps.

Like the rest of Britain in 1938-9, Orkney was bracing itself for renewed conflict. By the actual outbreak of war on 3 September 1939, however, only limited progress had been made in the creation of defences appropriate to the task of protecting the Home Fleet on its return to its principal wartime anchorage in Scapa Flow. Not only were there dangerously few defences in operational working order.

There was also insufficient appreciation of the fact that, as the setting for the interned German High Seas Fleet in 1918-19, the anchorage had now also acquired enhanced status as an enemy target, a symbol of humiliated German pride that was to be avenged at all costs. Thus for Orkney, unlike the much of the rest of Britain, there was to be no initial lull, no so-called 'phoney war'; from the outset it was subjected to devastating attack by air and sea.

Fear of the threat which torpedo-bearing submarines had come to pose to capital surface ships underpins the plot of The Spy in Black, book and film alike. Anti-submarine defences comprising lines of blockships and/or successive arrays of steel nets, minefields and indicator loops had kept these sinister vessels at bay during World War I. Many are known to have been effectively deterred and at least one, attempting to breach the southern defences in the last month of the war, was destroyed in a controlled minefield explosion. It took only six weeks of World War II, however, to turn into grim, tragic reality the threat which submarines posed and the fear which they instilled. On the night of 13-14 October 1939 the commander of U47 skilfully exploited the inadequacies of the blockship defences across the deepest of the vulnerable eastern channels into Scapa Flow, and then proceeded to torpedo and sink the 29,000-ton battleship

HMS Royal Oak at anchor off Gaitnip, just a few sea miles to the east of Smoogro, with the loss of 833 lives.

It goes without saying that suspicions of espionage became attached to this episode. Whatever shadows may still lurk behind those suspicions, the simple truth is that it took a traumatic event of this magnitude to focus the minds of defence chiefs and politicians at the highest levels. Confronted with a clear-cut strategic option of abandoning Scapa Flow altogether, they decided to try and render it impregnable. By mid-1940 it had indeed become, to use Churchill's term, a fortress 'home' for the Home Fleet. Its defences against air and sea attack were for a time more densely concentrated than anywhere else in Britain outside London.

No less than 25 heavy anti-aircraft batteries formed the nucleus of the system of aerial defences which proved capable of mounting sheets of fire famously known as the Scapa 'box barrage'. Five of these very considerable four-gun batteries were ranged along the north shore of the Flow, including a pair close together at Smoogro, just a few hundred yards to the landward of Smoogro House.

The installations of war – bigger, noisier and busier than ever before – had thus once more arrived on the doorstep of the author's residence. But just what he made of them in his last years before his death in 1944 is not recorded.

Geoffrey Stell is an architectural historian with specialist interests in Scottish architecture and fortifications. He is the former Head of Architecture at the Royal Commission on the Ancient and Historical Monuments of Scotland and is now an Honorary Lecturer in the Department of History, University of Stirling, and Visiting Lecturer in the Department of Architecture, Edinburgh College of Art. Author of numerous books and articles, he is currently engaged in, among other things, the preparation of The Defences of Scotland, to be published by Birlinn, and a series of 12 regional reports on 20th-century defences for Historic Scotland.

The Spy In Black

By Joseph Storer Clouston

PART 1

THE NARRATIVE OF LIEUTENANT VON BELKE
(OF THE GERMAN NAVY).

I. – THE LANDING

IF ANYONE had been watching the bay that August night (which, fortunately for us, there was not), they would have seen up till an hour after midnight as lonely and peaceful a scene as if it had been some inlet in Greenland. The war might have been waging on another planet. The segment of a waning moon was just rising, but the sky was covered with clouds, except right overhead where a bevy of stars twinkled, and it was a dim though not a dark night. The sea was as flat and calm as you can ever get on an Atlantic coast – a glassy surface, but always a gentle regular bursting of foam upon the beach. In a semicircle the shore rose black, towering at either horn (and especially on the south) into high dark cliffs.

I suppose a bird or two may have been crying then as they were a little later, but there was not a light nor a sign of anything human being within a hundred miles. If one of the Vikings who used to live in those islands had revisited that particular glimpse of the moon, he could never have guessed that his old haunts had altered a tittle. But if he had waited a while he would have rubbed his eyes and wondered. Right between the headlands he would have seen it dimly: – a great thing that was not a fish rising out of the calm water, and then very stealthily creeping in and in towards the southern shore.

When we were fairly on the surface I came on deck and gazed over the dark waters to the darker shore, with – I don't mind confessing it now – a rather curious sensation. To tell the truth, I was a little nervous, but I think I showed no sign of it to Wiedermann.

" You have thought of everything you can possibly need?" he asked in a low voice.

"Everything, sir, I think," I answered confidently.

"No need to give you tips!" he said with a laugh.

I felt flattered – but still my heart was beating just a little faster than usual!

In we crept closer and closer, with the gentlest pulsation of our engines that could not have been heard above the lapping of the waves on the pebbles. An invisible gull or two wheeled and cried above us, but otherwise there was an almost too perfect stillness. I could not help an uncomfortable suspicion that *some one* was watching. *Some one* would soon be giving the alarm, *some one* would presently be playing the devil with my schemes. It was sheer nonsense, but then I had never played the spy before – at least, not in war-time.

Along the middle of the bay ran a beach of sand and pebbles, with dunes and grass links above, but at the southern end the water was deep close inshore, and there were several convenient ledges of rock between the end of this beach and the beginning of the cliffs. The submarine came in as close as she dared, and then, without an instant's delay, the boat was launched. Wiedermann, myself, two sailors, and the motor-bicycle just managed to squeeze in, and we cautiously pulled for the ledges.

The tide was just right (we had thought of everything, I must say that), and after a minute or two's groping along the rocks, we found a capital landing. Wiedermann and I jumped ashore as easily as if it had been a quay, and my bicycle should have been landed without a hitch. How it happened I know not, but just as the sailors were lifting it out, the boat swayed a little and one of the clumsy fellows let his end of it slip. A splash of spray broke over it; a mere nothing, it seemed at the time, and then I had hold of it and we lifted it on to the ledge.

Wiedermann spoke sharply to the man, but I assured him no harm had been done, and between us we wheeled the thing over the flat rocks, and pulled it up to the top of the grass bank beyond.

"I can manage all right by myself now," I said. "Goodbye, sir!"

He gave my hand a hard clasp.

"This is Thursday night," he said. "We shall be back on Sunday, Monday, and Tuesday nights, remember."

"The British Navy and the weather permitting!" I laughed.

"Do not fear!" said he. "I shall be here, and we shall get you aboard somehow. Come any one of those nights that suits *him*."

"That suits him?" I laughed. "Say rather that suits Providence!"

"Well," he repeated, "I'll be here anyhow. Good luck!" We saluted, and I started on my way, wheeling my bicycle over the grass. I confess, however, that I had not gone many yards before I stopped and looked back. Wiedermann had disappeared from the top of the bank, and in a moment I heard the faint sounds of the boat rowing back. Very dimly against the grey sea I could just pick out the conning tower and low side of the submarine. The gulls were still crying, but in a more sombre key, I fancied.

So here was I, Conrad von Belke, lieutenant in the German Navy, treading British turf underfoot, cut off from any hope of escape for three full days at least! And it was not ordinary British turf either. I was on the holy of holies, actually landed on those sacred, jealously-guarded islands (which, I presume, I must not even name here), where the Grand Fleet had its lair. As to the mere act of landing, well, you have just seen that there was no insuperable difficulty in stepping ashore from a submarine at certain places, if the conditions were favourable and the moment cunningly chosen; but I proposed to penetrate to the innermost sanctuary, and spend at least three days there – a very different proposition!

I had been chosen for this service for three reasons: because I was supposed to be a cool hand in what the English call a "tight place"; because I could talk English not merely fluently, but with the real accent and intonation – like a native, in fact; and I believe because they thought me not quite a fool. As you shall hear, there was to be one much wiser than I to guide me. He was indeed the brain of this desperate enterprise, and I but his messenger and assistant. Still, one wants a messenger with certain qualities, and as it is the chief object of this narrative to clear my honour in the eyes of those who sent me, I wish to point out that they deliberately chose me for this job – I did not select myself – and that I did my best.

It was my own idea to take a motor-bicycle, but it was an idea cordially approved by those above me. There were several obvious advantages. A motor-cyclist is not an uncommon object on the roads even of those out-of-the-way islands, so that my mere appearance would attract no suspicion; and besides, they would scarcely expect a visitor of my sort to come ashore equipped with such an article. Also, I would cover the ground quickly, and, if it came to the worst, might have a chance of evading pursuit. But there was one reason which particularly appealed to me: I could wear my naval uniform underneath a suit of cyclist's overalls, and so if I were caught might make a strong plea to escape the fate of a spy; in fact, I told myself I was not a spy, – simply a venturesome scout. Whether the British would take the same view of me was another question! Still, the motor-cycle did give me a chance.

My first task was to cover the better part of twenty miles before daybreak and join forces with "him" in the very innermost shrine of this sanctuary – or rather, on the shore of it. This seemed a simple enough job; I had plenty of time, the roads, I knew, were good, nobody would be stirring (or anyhow, ought to be) at that hour, and the arrangements for my safe reception were, as you shall hear, remarkably ingenious. If I once struck the hard main road, I really saw nothing that could stop me.

The first thing was to strike this road. Of course I knew the map by heart, and had a copy in my pocket as a precaution that was almost superfluous, but working by map-memory in the dark is not so easy when one is going across country.

The grassy bank fell gently before me as the land sloped down from the cliffs to the beach, and I knew that within a couple of hundred yards I should find a rough road which followed the shore for a short way, and then when it reached the links above the beach, turned at right angles across them to join the highroad. Accordingly I bumped my motor-cycle patiently over the rough grass, keeping close to the edge of the bank so as to guide myself, and every now and then making a detour of a few yards inland to see whether the road had begun. The minutes passed, the ground kept falling till I was but a little above the level of the glimmering sea, the road ought to have begun to keep me company long ago, but never a sign of it could I find. Twice in my detours I stumbled into what seemed sand-holes, and turned back out of them sharply. And then at last I realised that I had ceased to descend for the last hundred yards or more, and in fact must be on the broad stretch of undulating sea links that fringed the head of the bay. But where was my road?

I stopped, bade myself keep quite cool and composed, and peered round me into the night. The moon was farther up and it had become a little lighter, but the clouds still obscured most of the sky and it was not light enough to see much. Overhead were the stars; on one hand the pale sea merged into the dark horizon; all around me were low black hummocks that seem to fade into an infinity of shadows. The gulls still cried mournfully, and a strong pungent odour of seaweed filled the night air. I remember that pause very vividly.

I should have been reckless enough to light a cigarette had I not feared that our submarine might still be on the surface, and Wiedermann might see the flash and dub me an idiot. I certainly needed a smoke very badly and took some credit to myself for refraining (though perhaps I ought really have given it to Wiedermann). And then I decided to turn back, slanting, however, a little away from the sea so as to try and cut across the road. A minute or two later I tumbled into a small chasm and came down with the bicycle on top of me. I had found my road.

The fact was that the thing, though marked on the largescale map as a road of the third, fourth, or tenth quality (I forget which), was actually nothing more or less than three parallel crevasses in the turf filled with loose sand. It was into these crevasses that I had twice stumbled already.

Now with my back to the sea and keeping a yard or two away from this wretched track, but with its white sand to guide me, I pushed my motor-cycle laboriously over the rough turf for what seemed the better part of half an hour. In reality I suppose it was under ten minutes, but with the night passing and that long ride before me, I never want a more patience-testing job. And then suddenly the white sand ceased. I stepped across to see what was the matter, and found myself on a hard highroad. It was a branch of the main road that led towards the shore, and for the moment I had quite forgotten its existence. I could have shouted for joy.

" Now," I said to myself, "I'm off!"

And off I went, phut-phut-phutting through the cool night air, with a heart extraordinarily lightened. That little bit of trouble at the start had made the rest of the whole wild enterprise seem quite simple now that it was safely over.

I reached the end of this branch, swung round to the right into the highroad proper and buzzed along like a tornado. The sea by this time had vanished, but I saw the glimmer of a loch on my left, and close at hand low walls and dim vistas of cultivated fields. A dark low building whizzed by, and then a gaunt eerie-looking standing stone, and then came a dip and beyond it a little rise in the ground. As I took this rise there suddenly came upon me a terrible sinking of the heart. Phut-phut! went my cycle, loudly and emphatically, and then came a horrible pause. Phut! once more; then two or three feeble explosions, and then silence. My way stopped; I threw over my leg and landed on the road.

"What the devil!" I muttered.

I had cleaned the thing, oiled it, seen that everything was in order; what in heaven's name could be the matter? And then with a dreadful sensation I remembered that wave of salt water.

II. – Night in the Ruined House

You may smile to think of a sailor being dismayed by a splash of salt water; but not if you are a motor-cyclist! Several very diabolical consequences may ensue.

In the middle of that empty road, in that alien land, under the hostile stars, I took my electric torch and endeavoured to discover what was the matter. From the moment I remembered the probable salt, wet cause of my mishap I had a pretty hopeless feeling. At the end of ten minutes I felt not merely quite hopeless, but utterly helpless. Helpless as a child before a charging elephant, hopeless as a man at the bottom of an Alpine crevasse. Ignition, carburettor, what had been damaged? In good daylight it might take me an hour or two first to discover and then to mend. By the radiance of my torch I would probably spend a night or two, and be none the wiser.

And meantime the precious dark hours were slipping away, and scattered all over the miles of country lay foemen sleeping – nothing but foes. I was in a sea-girt isle with but one solitary friend, and he was nearly twenty miles away, and I had the strictest orders not to approach him save under the cover of darkness. Enough cause for a few pretty black moments, I think you will allow.

And then I took myself by the scruff of the neck and gave myself a hearty shake. Had I been picked for this errand because I was a coward or a resourceless fool? No! Well, then, I must keep my head and use my wits, and if I could not achieve the best thing, I must try to do the second best. I ran over all the factors in the problem.

Firstly, to wait in the middle of that road trying to accomplish a job which I knew perfectly well it was a thousand chances to one against my managing, was sheer perverse folly.

Secondly, to leave my cycle in a ditch and try to cover the distance on my own two legs before daybreak was a physical impossibility. My cycle being one of the modern kind with no pedals, I could not even essay the dreadful task of grinding it along with my feet. Therefore I could not reach my haven to-night by any conceivable means.

On the other hand, I would still be expected to-morrow night, for our plans were laid to allow something for mischances; so if I could conceal myself and my cycle through the coming day, all might yet be well. Therefore I must devise some plan for concealing myself.

Logic had brought me beautifully so far, but now came the rub – Where was I to hide? These islands, you may or may not know, are to all practical purposes treeless and hedgeless. They have many moors and waste places, but of an abominable kind for a fugitive – especially a fugitive with a motor-cycle. The slopes are long and usually gentle and quite exposed; ravines and dells are few and far between and farther still to reach. Caves and clefts among the rocks might be found no doubt, but I should probably break my neck looking for them in the dark. Conceive of a man with a motor-bicycle looking for a cave by starlight!

And then a heaven-sent inspiration visited me. On board we had of course maps with every house marked, however small, and who lived in it, and so on. We do things thoroughly, even though at the moment there may not be any apparent reason for some of the details. I blessed our system now, for suddenly in my mind's eye I saw a certain group of farm buildings marked "ruinous and uninhabited." And now where the devil was it?

My own pocket map of course had no such minute details and I had to work my memory hard. And then in a flash I saw the map as distinctly as if it had really been under my eye instead of safely under the Atlantic.

"I have a chance still!" I said to myself.

By the light of my torch I had a careful look at my small map, and then I set forth pushing my lifeless cycle. To get to my refuge I had to turn back and retrace my steps (or perhaps I should rather say my revolutions) part way to the shore till I came to a road branching southwards, roughly parallel to the coast. It ascended continuously and pretty steeply, and I can assure you it was stiff work pushing a motor-cycle up that interminable hill, especially when one was clad for warmth and not for exercise. Dimly in the waxing moonlight I could see low farm buildings here and there, but luckily not a light shone nor a dog barked from one of them. Glancing over my shoulder I saw the sea, now quite distinct and with a faint sheen upon its surface, widening and widening as I rose. But I merely glanced at it enviously and concentrated my attention on the task of finding my "ruinous and uninhabited" farm.

I twice nearly turned off the road too soon, but I did find it at last – a low tumble-down group of little buildings some two hundred yards or so off the road on the right, or seaward side. Here the cultivated fields stopped, and beyond them the road ascended through barren moorland. My refuge was, in fact, the very last of the farms as one went up the hill. It lay pretty isolated from the others, and there was a track leading to it that enabled me to push my cycle along fairly comfortably.

"I might have come to a much worse place!" I said to myself hopefully.

Though there was not a sign of life about the place, and not a sound of any kind, I still proceeded warily, as I explored the derelict farm. I dared not even use my torch till I had stooped through an open door, and was safely within one of the buildings. When I flashed it round me I saw then that I stood in a small and absolutely empty room, which might at one time have been anything from a parlour to a byre, but now seemed consecrated to the cultivation of nettles. It had part of a roof overhead, and seemed as likely to suit my purpose as any other of the dilapidated group, so I brought my cycle in, flattened a square yard or two of nettles, and sat down on the floor with my back against the wall. And then I lit a cigarette and meditated.

"My young friend," I said to myself, "you are in an awkward position, but, remember, you have been in awkward positions before when there were no such compensating advantages! Let us consider these advantages and grow cheerful. You are privileged to render your country such a service as few single Germans have been able to render her – if this plan succeeds! If it fails, your sacrifice will not be unknown or unappreciated. Whatever happens, you will have climbed a rung or two up the ladder of duty, and perhaps of fame."

This eloquence pleased my young friend so much that he lit another cigarette.

"Consider again," I resumed, "what an opportunity you have been unexpectedly presented with for exhibiting your resourcefulness and your coolness and your nerve! If it had not been for that wave of salt water your task would have been almost too simple. Your own share of the enterprise would merely have consisted in a couple of easy rides on a motor-cycle, and perhaps the giving of a few suggestions, or the making of a few objections, which would probably have been brushed aside as worthless. *Now* you have really something to test you!"

This oration produced a less exhilarating effect. In fact, it set me to wondering very gravely how I could best justify this implied tribute to my powers of surmounting difficulties. Till the day broke all I had to do was to sit still, but after that – what? I pondered for a few minutes, and then I came to the conclusion that an hour or two's sleep would probably freshen my wits. I knew I could count on waking when the sun rose, and so I closed my eyes' and presently was fast asleep.

When I awoke, it was broad daylight. Looking first through the pane-less window and then through the gap in the roof, I saw that it was a grey, still morning that held promise of a fine day, though whether that was to my advantage or disadvantage I did not feel quite sure. Nobody seemed to be stirring yet about the houses or fields, so I had still time for deliberation before fate forced my hand.

First of all, I had a look round my immediate surroundings. I was well sheltered, as all the walls were standing, and there was most of a roof over my head (the last being a point of some importance in case any aircraft chanced to make a flight in this direction). It is true that the door was gone, but even here I seemed fortunate, for another small building, also dilapidated-looking but in somewhat better condition stood right opposite the open doorway and hid it completely. This little building still had a dishevelled door which stood closed, and for a moment I half thought of changing my shelter and taking possession of it; and then I decided that where fate had directed my steps, there should I abide.

The next thing obviously was to overhaul my motorcycle, and this I set about at once, though all the time my thoughts kept working. In the course of an hour or so I had located the trouble in the carburettor and put it right again, and I had also begun to realise a few of the pros and cons of the situation.

I now ate a few sandwiches, had a pull at my flask, lit a cigarette, and put the case to myself squarely.

"With a motor-cycle, the whole island at my disposal, and daylight in which to search it through, I can surely find a hiding-place a little farther removed from inquisitive neighbours," I said to myself. "So the sooner I am off the better."

But then I answered back-

"On the other hand it may take me some hours to find a better spot than this, and a man tearing about the country on a motor-cycle is decidedly more conspicuous in the early morning than in the middle of the day or the afternoon when cyclists are natural objects.

"But again, if I do think of leaving this place I certainly ought not to be seen in the act of emerging from a ruinous house pushing my cycle – not, at least, if I wish to be considered a normal feature of the landscape. I have a chance of escaping now unobserved; shall I have such a chance later in the day?"

Finally I decided to compromise. I should stay where I was till the hour when all the farmers had their mid-day meal. Then I might well hope to slip out unobserved, and thereafter scour the country looking for the ideal hiding-place without attracting any particular attention. But whatever merits this scheme may have had were destined never to be tested.

From my seat amid the nettles I could see right through the open door, and my eyes all this while were resting on the glimpse of grey building outside. All at once I held my breath, and the hand that was lifting a cigarette to my lips grew rigid. A thin wisp of smoke was rising from the chimney.

III. – BEHIND THE WALL.

" RUINOUS" these farm buildings certainly were; but "uninhabited" – obviously not quite! I rose stealthily and crossed to the door, and just as I reached it the door of the other house began to open. I stepped back and peered round the corner for quite a minute before anything more happened. My neighbour, whoever he was, seemed unconscionably slow in his movements.

And then a very old, bent, and withered woman appeared, with a grey shawl about her head. As she looked slowly round her, first to one side and then to the other, I cautiously drew back; but even as I did so I knew it was too late. A wisp of smoke had given us both away. This time it was a trail from my cigarette which I could see quite plainly drifting through the open door.

I heard her steps coming towards me, and then her shadow filled the doorway. There was nothing for it but taking the bull by the horns.

"Good morning!" I said genially.

She did not start. She did not speak. She just stared at me out of as unpleasant-looking a pair of old eyes as I have ever looked into. I suspected at once why the old crone lived here by herself; she did not look as if she would be popular among her neighbours.

"I think it is going to be a fine day," I continued breezily.

She simply continued to stare; and if ever I saw suspicion in human eyes, I saw it in hers.

"What do you think yourself?" I inquired with a smile. "I have no doubt you are more weatherwise than I."

Then at last she spoke, and I thought I had never heard a more sinister remark.

"Maybe it will be a fine day for some," she replied.

"I hope I may be one of them!" I said as cheerfully as possible.

She said not one word in reply, and her silence completed the ominous innuendo.

It struck me that a word of explanation would be advisable. "My bicycle broke down," I said, "and I took the liberty of bringing it in here to repair it."

Her baleful gaze turned upon my hapless motor-cycle.

"What for did you have to mend it in here?" she inquired; very pertinently, I could not but admit.

"It was the most convenient place I could find," I replied carelessly.

"To keep it from the rain maybe?" she suggested.

"Well," I admitted, "a roof has some advantages."

"Then," said she, "you've been here a long while, for there's been no rain since I wakened up."

"But I didn't say I came here for shelter," I said hastily. She stared at me again for a few moments.

"You're saying first one thing and then the other," she pronounced.

I felt inclined to tell her that she had missed her vocation. What a terrible specimen of the brow-beating, cross-examining lawyer she would have made! However, I decided that my safest line was cheerful politeness.

"Have it your own way, my good dame!" I said lightly. Her evil eyes transfixed me.

"You'll be a foreigner," she said.

"A foreigner!" I exclaimed; "why on earth should you think that?"

"You're using queer words," she replied. "What words?" I demanded.

"Dame is the German for an old woman," said she.

This astonishing philological discovery might have amused me at another time, but at this moment it only showed me too clearly how her thoughts were running.

" Well," said I, "if it's German, I can only say it is the first word of that beastly language I've ever spoken!" Again I was answered by a very ominous silence. It occurred to me very forcibly that the sooner I removed myself from this neighbourhood the better.

"Well," I said, "my bicycle is mended now, so I had better be off."

"You had that," she agreed.

"Good-bye!" I cried as I led my cycle out, but she never spoke a syllable in reply.

"Fate has not lost much time in forcing my hand!" I said to myself as I pushed my motor-cycle along the track towards the highroad. I thought it wiser not to look round, but just before I reached the road I glanced over my left shoulder, and there was the old woman crossing the fields at a much brisker pace than I should have given her credit for, and heading straight for the nearest farm. My hand was being forced with a vengeance.

Instinctively I should liked to have turned uphill and got clear of this district immediately, but I was not sure how my cycle would behave itself, and dared not risk a stiff ascent to begin with. So I set off at top speed down the road I had come the night before, passing the old crone at a little distance off, and noticing more than one labourer in the fields or woman at a house door, staring with interest at this early morning rider. When the news had spread of where he had come from, and with what language he interlarded his speech, they might do something more than stare. There was a telegraph-office not at all far away.

As I sped down that hill and swung round away from the sea at the foot, I did a heap of quick thinking. As things had turned out I dared not make for any place of concealment far off the highroads. Now that there was a probability of the hue and cry being raised, or at least of a look-out being kept for me, the chances of successfully slipping up the valley of some burn without anyone's notice were enormously decreased. I had but to glance round at the openness of the countryside to realise that. No; on the highroads I could at least run away, but up in the moors I should be a mere trapped rat.

Then I had the bright thought of touring in zigzag fashion round and round the island, stopping every here and there to address an inhabitant and leave a false clue, so as to confuse my possible pursuers. But what about my petrol? I might need every drop if I actually did come to be chased. So I gave up that scheme.

Finally, I decided upon a plan which really seems to me now to be as promising as any I could think of. About the least likely place to look for me would be a few miles farther along the same road that ran past my last night's refuge, in the opposite direction from that in which people had seen me start. I resolved to make a detour and then work back to that road.

I had arrived at this decision by the time I reached the scene of last night's mishap. Fortunately my cycle was running like a deer now, and I swept up the little slope in a few seconds and sped round the loch, opening up fresh vistas of round-topped heather hills and wide green or brown valleys every minute. At a lonely bit of the road I jumped off, studied my map afresh, and then dashed on again.

Presently a side road opened, leading back towards the coast, and round the corner I sped; but even as I did so the utter hopelessness of my performance struck me vividly – that is to say, if a really serious and organised hunt for me were to be set afoot. For the roadside was dotted with houses, often at considerable intervals it is true, but then all of them had such confoundedly wide views over that open country. There was a house or two at the very corner where I turned, and I distinctly saw a face appearing at a window to watch me thunder past. The noise these motorcycles make is simply infernal!

It was then that I fell into the true spirit for such an adventure. Since the chances were everywhere against me *if* my enemies took certain steps, well then, the only thing to do was to hope they did not take them and dismiss that matter from my mind. I was taking the best precautions I could think of, and the cooler I kept and better spirits I was in, the more likely would luck be to follow me. For luck is a discerning lady and likes those who trust her. Accordingly, the sun being now out and the morning beautifully fine, I decided to enjoy the scenery and make the most of a day ashore.

My first step was to ease up and ride just as slowly as I could, and then I saw at once that I was doing the wisest thing in every way. I made less noise and less dust, and was altogether much less of a phenomenon. And this encouraged me greatly to keep to my new resolution.

"If I leave it all to luck, she will advise me well!" I said to myself.

I headed coastwards through a wide marshy valley with but few houses about, and in a short time saw the sea widening before me and presently struck the road I was seeking. At the junction I obeyed an impulse, and, jumping off my cycle, paused to survey the scenery. A fertile vale fell from where I stood, down to a small bay between headlands. It was filled with little farms, and all at once there came over me an extraordinary impression of peacefulness and rest. Could it actually be that this was a country at war; that naval war, indeed, was very, very close at hand, and beneath those shining waters a submarine might even now be stealing or a loose mine drifting? The wide, sunshiny, placid atmosphere of the scene, with its vast expanse of clear blue sky, larks singing high up and sea-birds crying about the shore, soothed my spirits like a magician's wand. I mounted and rode on again in an amazingly pleasant frame of mind for a spy within a hair's-breadth of capture, and very probably of ignominious death.

Up a long hill my engine gently throbbed, with moorland on either side that seemed to be so desolated by the gales and sea spray that even heather could scarcely flourish. I meant to stop and rest by the wayside, but after a look at the map I thought on the whole I had better put another mile or two between me and the lady with the baleful eyes. At the top I had a very wide prospect of inland country to the left, a treeless northern-looking scene, all green and brown with many lakes reflecting the sunshine. A more hopeless land to hide in I never beheld, and I was confirmed in my reckless resolution. Chance alone must protect me.

Down a still steeper hill I rode, only now amid numberless small farms and with another bay shining ahead. The road ran nearly straight into the water and then bent suddenly and followed the rim of the bay, with nothing but empty sea-links on the landward side. The farms were left behind, a mansion-house by the shore was still a little distance ahead, and there was not a living soul in sight as I came to a small stone-walled enclosure squeezed in between the road and the beach below. I jumped off, led my cycle round this and laid it on the ground, and then seated myself with my back against the low wall of loose stones and my feet almost projecting over the edge of the steep slope of pebbles that fell down to the sand.

I was only just out of sight, but unless anyone should walk along the beach, out of sight I certainly was, and it struck me forcibly that ever since I had given myself up to luck, every impulse had been an inspiration. If I were conducting the search for myself, would I ever dream of looking for the mysterious runaway behind a wall three feet high within twenty paces of a public road and absolutely exposed to a wide sweep of beach? "No," I told myself, "I certainly should not!"

There I sat for hour after hour basking in the sunshine, and yet despite my heavy clothing kept at a bearable temperature by gentle airs of cool breeze off the sea. The tide, which was pretty high when I arrived, crept slowly down the sands, but save for the cruising and running of gulls and little piping shore-birds, that was all the movement on the beach. Not a soul appeared below me all that time. The calm shining sea remained absolutely empty except once for quarter of an hour or so when a destroyer was creeping past far out. To the seaward there was not a hint of danger or the least cause for apprehension.

On the road behind me I did hear sounds several times, which I confess disturbed my equanimity much more than I meant to let them. Once a motor-car buzzed past, and not to hold my breath as the sound swelled so rapidly and formidably was more than I could achieve. The jogging of a horse and trap twice set me wondering, despite myself, whether there were a couple of men with carbines aboard. But the slow prolonged rattling and creaking of carts was perhaps the sound that worried me most. They took such an interminable time to pass! I conceived a very violent distaste for carts.

I do take some credit to myself that not once did I yield to the temptation to peep over my wall and see who it was that passed along the road. I did not even turn and try to peer through the chinks in the stones, but simply sat like a limpet till the sounds had died completely away. The only precaution I took was to extinguish my cigarette if I chanced at the moment to be smoking.

In the course of my long bask in that sun bath I ate most of my remaining sandwiches and a cake or two of chocolate, but kept the remainder against emergencies. At last as the sun wore round, gradually descending till it shone right into my eyes, and I realised that the afternoon was getting far through, hope began to rise higher and higher. It actually seemed as if I were going to be allowed to remain within twenty yards of a highroad till night fell. "And then let them look for me!" I thought.

I don't think my access of optimism caused me to make any incautious movement. I know I was not smoking, in fact it must simply have been luck determined to show me that I was not her only favourite. Anyhow, when I first heard a footstep it was on the grass within five yards of me, and the next moment a man came round the corner of the wall and stopped dead short at the sight of me.

He was a countryman, a small farmer or hired man, I should judge – a broad-faced, red-bearded, wide-shouldered, pleasant-looking fellow, and he must have been walking for some distance on the grass by the roadside, though what made him step the few yards out of his way to look round the corner of the wall, I have never discovered to this day. Possibly he meant to descend to the beach at that point. Anyhow there he was, and as we looked into one another's eyes for a moment in silence I could tell as surely as if he had said the words that he had heard the story of the suspicious motor-cyclist.

IV. – THE NAILS.

" A FINE afternoon," I remarked, without rising, and I hope without showing any sign of emotion other than pleasure at making an acquaintance.

" Aye," said he, briefly and warily.

This discouraging manner was very ominous, for the man was as good-natured and agreeable-looking a fellow as I ever met.

"The weather looks like keeping up," I said.

He continued to look at me steadily, and made no answer at all this time. Then he turned his back to me very deliberately, lifted his felt hat, and waved it two or three times round his head, evidently to some one in the distance. I saw instantly that mischief was afoot and time precious, yet the fellow was evidently determined and stout-hearted, besides being physically very powerful, and it would never do to rouse his suspicions to the pitch of grappling with me. Of course I might use my revolver, but I had no wish to add a civilian's death to the other charge I might have to face before that sun had set. Suddenly luck served me well again by putting into my head a well-known English cant phrase.

"Are you often taken like that?" I inquired with a smile. He turned round again and stared blankly. I imitated the movement of waving a hat, and laughed.

"Or is it a family custom?" I asked.

He was utterly taken aback, and looked rather foolish. I sat still and continued to smile at him. And then he broke into a smile himself.

"I was just waving on a friend," he explained, and I could detect a note of apology in his voice. For the moment he was completely hoodwinked. How long it would last Heaven knew, but I clearly could not afford to imitate Mr Asquith, and "wait and see."

"Oh," I said with a laugh, "I see!"

And then I glanced at my wristlet watch, and sprang to my feet with an exclamation.

" By Jove, I'll be late!" I said, and picking up my cycle wheeled it briskly to the road, remarking genially as I went, "the days are not so long as they were!"

I never saw a man more obviously divided in mind. Was I the suspicious person he fancied at first? Or was I an honest and peaceable gentleman? Meanwhile I had cast one brief but sufficient glance along the road. Just at the foot of the steep hill down which I had come in the morning a man was mounting a motor-cycle. Beside him stood one or two others – country folk, so far as I could judge at the distance, and piecing things together, it seemed plain that my friend had lately been one of the party, and that the man they had been gossiping with was a motor-cyclist in search of me, who had actually paused to make inquiries within little over a quarter of a mile from where I sat. Quite possibly he had been there for some time, and almost certainly he would have ridden past without suspecting my presence if it had not been for the diabolical mishap of this chance encounter.

I had planted my cycle on the road, and was ready to mount before my friend had made up his mind what to do. Even then his procedure luckily lacked decision.

"Beg pardon, sir —!" he began, making a step towards me.

"Good evening!" I shouted, and the next instant the engine had started, and I was in my saddle.

Even then my pursuer had got up so much speed that he must surely have caught me had he not stopped to make inquiry of my late acquaintance. I was rounding a corner at the moment, and so was able to glance over my shoulder and see what was happening. The cyclist was then in the act of remounting, and I noted that he was in very dark clothes. It might or might not have been a uniform, but I fancied it was. Anyhow, I felt peculiarly little enthusiasm for making his acquaintance.

On I sped, working rapidly up to forty miles an hour, and quite careless now of any little sensation I might cause. I had sensations myself, and did not grudge them to other people. The road quickly left the coast and turned directly inland, and presently it began to wind along the edge of a long reedy stretch of water, with a steep bank above it on the other side. The windings gave me several chances of catching a glimpse of my pursuer, and I saw that I was gaining nothing; in fact, if anything he was overhauling me.

"I'll try them!" I said to myself.

"Them" were nails. Wiedermann had done me no more than justice in assuming I had come well provided against possible contingencies. Each of my side-pockets had a little packet of large-headed, sharp-pointed nails. I had several times thrown them experimentally on the floor of my cabin, and found that a gratifying number lay point upwards. I devoutly prayed they would behave as reasonably now.

This stretch of road was ideal for their use – narrow, and with not a house to give succour or a spectator to witness such a very suspicious performance. I threw a handful behind me, and at the next turn of the road glanced round to see results. The man was still going strong. I threw another handful and then a third, but after that the road ran straight for a space, and it was only when it bent to the right round the head of the loch that I was able to see him again. He had stopped far back, and was examining his tyres.

The shadows by this time were growing long, but there were still some hours before darkness would really shelter me, and in the meantime what was I to do with myself, and where to turn? Judging from the long time that had elapsed between my discovery in the early morning and the appearance of this cyclist at the very place which I had thought would be the last where they would seek me, the rest of the island had probably been searched and the hue and cry had died down by this time. So for some time I ought to he fairly safe anywhere: until, in fact, my pursuer had reached a telegraph office, and other scouts had then been collected and sent out. And if my man was an average human being, he would certainly waste a lot of precious time in trying to pump up his tyres or mend them before giving it up as a bad job and walking to a telegraph office.

That, in fact, was what he did, for in this open country I was able a few minutes later to see him in the far distance still stopping by that loch shore. But though I believe in trusting to chance, I like to give myself as many chances as possible. I knew where all the telegraph offices were, and one was a little nearer him than I quite liked. So half a mile farther on, at a quiet spot on a hill, I jumped off and swarmed up one of the telegraph-posts by the roadside, and then I took out of my pocket another happy inspiration. When I came down again, there was a gap in the wire.

There was now quite a good chance that I might retain my freedom till night fell, and if I could hold out so long as that – well, we should see what happened then! But what was to be done in the meantime? A strong temptation assailed me, and I yielded to it. I should get as near to my night's rendezvous as possible, and try to find some secluded spot there. It was not perhaps the very wisest thing to risk being seen there by daylight and bring suspicion on the neighbourhood where I meant to spend two or three days; but you will presently see why I was so strongly tempted. So great, in fact, was the temptation that till I got there I hardly thought of the risk.

I rode for a little longer through the same kind of undulating, loch-strewn inland country, and then I came again close to the sea. But it was not the open sea this time. It was a fairly wide sound that led from the ocean into a very important place, and immediately I began to see things. What things they were precisely I may not say, but they had to do with warfare, with making this sound about as easy for a hostile ship to get through, whether above the water or below, as a pane of glass is for a bluebottle. As I rode very leisurely, with my head half turned round all the while, I felt that my time was not wasted if I escaped safely, having seen simply what I now noted. For my eye could put interpretations on features that would convey nothing to the ordinary traveller.

Gradually up and up a long gentle incline I rode, with the sound falling below me and a mass of high dark hills rising beyond it. Behind me the sun was now low, and my shadow stretched long on the empty road ahead. For it was singularly empty, and the country-side was utterly peaceful; only at sea was there life-with death very close beside it. And now and then there rose at intervals a succession of dull, heavy sounds that made the earth quiver. I knew what they meant!

Then came a dip, and then a very steep long hill through moorland country. And then quite suddenly and abruptly I came to the top. It was a mere knife-edge, with the road instantly beginning to descend steeply on the other side, but I did not descend with the road. I jumped off and stared with bated breath.

Ahead of me and far below, a wide island-encircled sheet of water lay placid and smiling in the late afternoon sunshine. Strung along one side of it were lines of grey ships, with a little smoke rising from most of their funnels, but lying quite still and silent – as still and silent as the farms and fields on shore. Those distant patches of grey, with the thin drifts of smoke and the masts encrusted with small grey blobs rising out of their midst, those were the cause of all my country's troubles. But for them peace would have long since been dictated and a mightier German Empire would be towering above all other States in the world. How I hated – and yet (being a sailor myself) how I respected them! One solitary monster of this Armada was slowly moving across the land-locked basin. Parallel to her and far away moved a tiny vessel with a small square thing following her at an even distance, and the sun shining on this showed its colour red. Suddenly out of the monster shot a series of long bright flashes. Nothing else happened for several seconds, and then almost simultaneously "Boom! boom! boom!" hit my ear, and a group of tall white fountains sprang up around the distant red target. The Grand Fleet of England was preparing for" The Day"!

I knew the big vessel at a glance; I knew her, at least, as one of a certain four, and for some moments I watched her gunnery practice, too fascinated to stir. I noted how the fall of her shells was spread – in fact I noted several things; and then it occurred to me abruptly that I stood a remarkably good chance of having a wall at my back and a handkerchief over my eyes if I lingered in this open road much longer. And the plea that I was enjoying the excellent gun-practice made by H.M.S. Blank would scarcely be accepted as an extenuating circumstance!

I glanced quickly round, and then I realised how wonderfully luck was standing by me. At the summit of that hill there were naturally no houses, and as the descending road on either side made a sharp twist almost immediately, I stood quite invisible on my outlook tower. The road, moreover, ran through a kind of neck, with heather rising on either side; and in a moment I had hauled my cycle up the bank on the landward side, and was out of sight over the edge, even should any traveller appear.

After a few minutes' laborious dragging of my cycle I found myself in a small depression in the heather, where, by lying down, I could remain quite out of sight unless someone walked right into me – and it seemed improbable that anyone should take such a promenade with the good road so close at hand. By raising myself on my knees I could command the same engrossing view I had seen from the road, only I now also saw something of the country that sloped down to the sea; and with a thrill of exultation I realised that this prospect actually included our rendezvous.

V. – WAITING.

WHAT I saw when I cautiously peered over the rim of that little hollow was (beginning at the top) a vast expanse of pale-blue sky, with fleecy clouds down near the horizon already tinged with pink reflections from the sunset far off behind my back. Then came a shining glimpse of the North Sea; then a rim of green islands, rising on the right to high heather hills; then the land-locked waters and the grey ships now getting blurred and less distinct; then some portions of the green land that sloped up to where I lay; and among these fields, and not far away from me, the steep roof and gable-top of a grey, old-fashioned house. It was the parish manse, the pacific abode of the professional exponent and exemplar of peace – the parish minister; and yet, curiously enough, it was that house which my eyes devoured.

The single ship had now ceased firing and anchored with her consorts, the fleet had grown too indistinct to note anything of its composition, and there was nothing to distract my attention from the house. I looked at it hard and long and studied the lie of the ground between it and me, and then I lay down on a couch of soft heather and began to think.

So far as I could see I had done nothing yet to draw suspicion to this particular spot, for no one at all seemed to have seen me, but it was manifest that there would be a hard and close hunt for the mysterious motor-cyclist on the morrow. I began to half regret that I had cut that telegraph wire and advertised myself so patently for what I was. Now it was quite obvious that for some days to come motorcycling would be an unhealthy pastime in these islands. Even at night how many ears would be listening for my 'phut-phut-phut,' and how many eyes would be scanning the dark roads? A few judiciously placed and very simple barricades – a mere bar on two uprights, with a sentry beside each – and what chance would I have of getting back to that distant bay, especially as I had just been seen so near it?

"However," I said to myself, "that is looking too far ahead. It was not my fault I brought this hornet's nest about my ears. Just bad luck and a clumsy sailor!"

Just then I heard something approaching on the road below me, and in a minute or two it became unmistakably the sound of a horse and trap. At one place I could catch a glimpse of this road between the hummocks of heather, and I raised myself again and looked out. In a moment the horse and trap appeared and I got a sensation I shall not soon forget. Not that there seemed to the casual passer-by anything in the least sensational about this equipage. He would merely have noticed that it contained, besides the driver, a few articles of luggage and a gentleman in a flat-looking felt hat and an overcoat – both of them black. This gentleman was sitting with his back to me (he was in a small waggonette), but I could scarcely doubt who it was. But only arriving to-night!

Curiosity and anxiety so devoured me that I ran a little risk. Getting out of my hollow, I crawled forward on my hands and knees till I could catch a glimpse of the side road leading to that house; and there I lay flat on my face and watched.

Down the steep hill the horse proceeded at a walk, and what between my impatience to make sure, and my consciousness of my own rashness in quitting even for a moment my sheltered hollow, I passed a few very uncomfortable minutes. The light by this time was failing fast, but it was quite clear enough to see (or be seen), and at last I caught one more glimpse of that horse and trap – turning off the road just where I expected. And then I was crawling back with more haste than dignity.

It was 'him'! And he had only arrived to-night. If it had not been for my accident, in what a nice dilemma I should have been landed! Never did I bless anyone more fervently than that awkward sailor who had let my cycle slip, and as for the wave of salt water which wet it, it seemed to have sprung from the age of miracles.

The trouble of my discovery and its possible consequences still remained, but I thought little enough of that now, so thankful did I feel for what had *not* happened. And then I stretched myself out again on the heather, waiting with all the patience I could muster for the falling of night.

PART II.

A FEW CHAPTERS BY THE EDITOR.

I. – THE PLEASANT STRANGER.

IT was in July of that same year that the Rev. Alexander Burnett was abashed to find himself inadvertently conspicuous. He had very heartily permitted himself to be photographed in the centre of a small group of lads from his parish who had heard their country's call and were home in their khaki for a last leave-taking. Moreover, the excellence of the photograph and the undeniably close resemblance of his own portrait to the reflection he surveyed each morning when shaving, had decidedly pleased him. But the appearance of this group, first as an illustration in a local paper and then in one that enjoyed a very wide circulation indeed, embarrassed him not a little. For he was a modest, publicity-avoiding man, and also he felt he ought to have been in khaki too.

Not that Mr Burnett had anything really to reproach himself with, for he was in the forties, some years above military age. But he was a widower without a family, who had already spent fifteen years in a sparsely inhabited parish in the south-east of Scotland not very far from the Border; and ever since he lost his wife had been uneasy in mind and a little morbid, and anxious for change of scene and fresh experiences. He was to get them, and little though he dreamt it, that group was their beginning. Indeed, it would have taken as cunning a brain to scent danger in the trifling incidents with which his strange adventure began as it took to arrange them. And Mr Burnett was not at all cunning, being a simple, quiet man. In appearance he was rather tall, with a clean-shaven, thoughtful face, and hair beginning to turn grey.

A few days later a newspaper arrived by post. He had received several already from well-meaning friends, each with that group in it, and he sighed as he opened this one. it was quite a different paper, however, with no illustrations, but with a certain page indicated in blue pencil, and a blue pencil mark in the margin of that page. What his attention was called to was simply the announcement that the Rev. Mr Maxwell, minister of the parish of Myredale, had been appointed to another charge, and that there was now a vacancy there.

Mr Burnett looked at the wrapper, but his name and address had been typewritten and gave him no clue. He wondered who had sent him the paper, and then his thoughts naturally turned to the vacant parish. He knew that it lay in a certain group of northern islands, which we may call here the Windy Isles, and he presumed that the stipend would not be great. Still, it was probably a better living than his own small parish, and as for its remoteness, well, he liked quiet out-of-the-way places, and it would certainly be a complete change of scene. He let the matter lie in the back of his mind, and there it would very likely have remained but for a curious circumstance on the following Sunday.

His little parish church was seldom visited by strangers, and when by any chance one did appear, the minister was very quickly conscious of the fact. He always took stock of his congregation during the first psalm, and on this Sabbath his experienced eye had noted a stranger before the end of the opening verse. A pleasant-looking gentleman in spectacles he appeared to be, and of a most exemplary and devout habit of mind. In fact he hardly once seemed to take his spectacled gaze off the minister's face during the whole service; and Mr Burnett believed in giving his congregation good measure.

It was a fine day, and when service was over the minister walked back to his manse at a very leisurely pace, enjoying the sunshine after a week of showery weather. The road he followed crossed the river, and as he approached the bridge he saw the same stranger leaning over the parapet, smoking a cigar, and gazing at the brown stream. Near him at the side of the road was drawn up a large dark-green touring car, which apparently the gentleman had driven himself, for there was no sign of a chauffeur.

"Good day, sir!" said the stranger affably, as the minister came up to him. "Lovely weather!"

Mr Burnett, nothing loath to hear a fresh voice, stopped and smiled and agreed that the day was fine. He saw now that the stranger was a middle-sized man with a full fair moustache, jovial eyes behind his gold-rimmed spectacles, and a rosy healthy colour; while his manner was friendliness itself. The minister felt pleasantly impressed with him at once.

"Any trout in this stream?" inquired the stranger.

Mr Burnett answered that it was famed as a fishing river, at which the stranger seemed vastly interested and pleased, and put several questions regarding the baskets that were caught. Then he grew a little more serious and said —

"I hope you will pardon me, sir, for thanking you for a very excellent sermon. As I happened to be motoring past just as church was going in I thought I'd look in too. But I assure you I had no suspicion I should hear so good a discourse. I appreciated it highly."

Though a modest man, Mr Burnett granted the stranger's pardon very readily. Indeed, he became more favourably impressed with him than ever.

"I am very pleased to hear you say so," he replied, "for in an out-of-the-way place like this one is apt to get very rusty."

"I don't agree with you at all, sir," said the stranger energetically, "if you'll pardon me saying so. In my experience — which is pretty wide, I may add — the best thinking is done in out-of-the-way places. I don't say the showiest, mind you, but the *best*!"

Again the minister pardoned him without difficulty.

"Of course, one needs a change now and then, I admit," continued the stranger. "But, my dear sir, whatever you do, don't go and bury yourself in a crowd!"

This struck Mr Burnett as a novel and very interesting way of putting the matter. He forgot all about the dinner awaiting him at the manse, and when the stranger offered him a very promising-looking cigar, he accepted it with pleasure, and leaned over the parapet beside him. There, with his eyes on the running water, he listened and talked for some time.

The stranger began to talk about the various charming out-of-the-way places in Scotland. It seemed he was a perfervid admirer of everything Scottish, and had motored or tramped all over the country from Berwick to the Pentland Firth. In fact, he had even crossed the waters, for he presently burst forth into a eulogy of the Windy Islands.

"The most delightful spot, sir, I have ever visited!" he said most enthusiastically. "There is a peacefulness and charm, and at the same time something stimulating in the air I simply can't describe. In body and mind I felt a new man after a week there!"

The minister was so clearly struck by this, and his interest so roused, that the stranger pursued the topic and added a number of enticing details.

"By the way," he exclaimed presently, "Do you happen to know a fellow-clergyman there called Maxwell? His parish is – let me see – Ah, Myredale, that's the name."

This struck Mr Burnett as quite extraordinary.

"I don't know him personally," he began.

"A very sensible fellow," continued the stranger impetuously. "He told me his parish was as like heaven as anything on this mortal earth!"

"He has just left it," said Mr Burnett.

The stranger seemed surprised and interested.

"What a chance for some one!" he exclaimed.

Mr Burnett gazed thoughtfully through the smoke of his cigar into the brown water of the river below him.

"I have had thoughts of making a change myself," he said slowly. "But of course they might not select me even if I applied for Myredale."

"In the Scottish Church the custom is to go to the vacant parish to preach a trial sermon, isn't it?" inquired the stranger.

The minister nodded. "A system I disapprove of, I may say," said he.

"I quite agree with you," said the stranger sympathetically. "Still, so long as that is the system, why not try your luck? Mind you, I talk as one who knows the place, and knows Mr Maxwell and his opinion of it. You'll have an enviable visit, whatever happens."

"It is a very long way," said Mr Burnett.

"Don't they pay your expenses?"

"Yes," admitted the minister. "But then I understand that those islands are very difficult for a stranger to enter at present. The naval authorities are extremely strict."

The stranger laughed jovially.

"My dear sir," he cried, "can you imagine even the British Navy standing between a Scotch congregation and its sermon! You are the one kind of stranger who will be admitted. All you have to do is to get a passport — and there you are!"

"Are they difficult to get?"

The stranger laughed again.

"I know nothing about that kind of thing," said he. "I'm a Lancashire lad, and the buzz of machinery is my game; but I can sagely say this: that *you* will have no difficulty getting a passport."

Mr Burnett again gazed at the water in silence.

Then he looked up and said with a serious face —

"I must really tell you, sir, of a very remarkable coincidence. Only a few days ago some unknown friend sent me a copy of a newspaper with a notice of this very vacancy marked in it!"

The Lancashire lad looked almost thunder-struck by this extraordinay disclosure.

"Well I'm hanged!" he cried – adding hurriedly, "if you'll forgive my strong language, sir."

"It seems to me to be providential," said Mr Burnett in a low and very serious voice.

With equal solemnity the stranger declared that though not an unusually good man himself, this solution had already struck him forcibly.

At this point the minister became conscious of the distant ringing of a bell, and recognised with a start the strident note of his own dinner bell swung with a vigorous arm somewhere in the road ahead. He shook hands cordially with the stranger, thanked him for the very interesting talk he had enjoyed, and hurried off towards his over-cooked roast.

The stranger remained for a few moments still leaning against the parapet. His jovial face had been wreathed in smiles throughout the whole conversation; he still smiled now, but with rather a different expression.

II. – THE CHAUFFEUR.

MR BURNETT was somewhat slow in coming to decisions, but once he had taken an idea to do a thing he generally carried it out. In the course of a week or ten days he had presented himself as a candidate for the vacant church of Myredale, and made arrangements for appearing in the pulpit there on a certain Sunday in August. He was to arrive in the islands on the Thursday, spend the week-end in the empty manse, preach on Sunday, and return on Monday or Tuesday. His old friend Mr Drummond in Edinburgh, hearing of the plan, invited him to break his journey at his house, arriving on Tuesday afternoon, and going on by the North train on Wednesday night. Accordingly, he arranged to have a trap at the manse on Tuesday afternoon, drive to Berwick and catch the Scotch express, getting into Edinburgh at 6.15.

He was a reticent man, and in any case had few neighbours to gossip with, so that as far as he himself knew, the Drummonds alone had been informed of all these details. But he had in the manse a very valuable domestic, who added to her more ordinary virtues a passion for conversation.

On the Saturday afternoon before he was due to start, he was returning from a walk, when he caught a glimpse of a man's figure disappearing into a small pine wood at the back of his house, and when his invaluable Mary brought him in his tea, he inquired who her visitor had been.

"Oh, sic a nice young felly!" said Mary enthusiastically. "He's been a soger, wounded at Mons he was, and walking to Berwick to look for a job."

Though simple, the minister was not without some sad experience of human nature, particularly the nature of wounded heroes, tramping the country for jobs.

"I hope you didn't give him any money," said he.

"He never askit for money!" cried Mary. "Oh, he was not that kind at a'! A maist civil young chap he was, and maist interested to hear where you were gaun, and sic like."

The minister shook his head.

"You told him when I was leaving, and all about it, I suppose?"

"There was nae secret, was there?" demanded Mary. Mr Burnett looked at her seriously.

"As like as not," said he; "he just wished to know when the man of the house would be away. Mind and keep the doors locked, Mary, and if he comes back, don't let him into the kitchen whatever cock-and-bull story he tells."

He knew that Mary was a sensible enough woman, and having given her this warning, he forgot the whole incident – till later.

Tuesday was fine and warm, a perfect day on which to start a journey, and about mid-day Mr Burnett was packing a couple of bags with a sense of pleasant anticipation, when a telegram arrived. This was exactly how it ran:-

" My friend Taylor motoring to Edinburgh to-day. Will pick you and luggage up at Manse about six, and bring you to my house. Don't trouble reply, assume this suits, shall be out till late.

"DRUMMOND."

"There's no answer," said Mr Burnett with a smile.

He was delighted with this change in his programme, and at once countermanded his trap, and ordered Mary to set about making scones and a currant cake for tea.

"This Mr Taylor will surely be wanting his tea before he starts," said he, "though it's likely he won't want to waste too much time over it, or it will be dark long before we get to Edinburgh. So have everything ready, Mary, but just the infusing of the tea."

Then with an easy mind, feeling that there was no hurry now, he sat down to his early dinner. As he dined he studied the telegram more carefully, and it was then that one or two slight peculiarities struck him. They seemed to him very trifling, but they set him wondering and smiling a little to himself.

He knew most of the Drummonds' friends, and yet never before had he heard of an affluent motor-driving Mr Taylor among them. Still, there was nothing surprising about that, for one may make a new friend any day, and one's old friends never hear of him for long enough.

The really unusual features about this telegram were its length and clearness and the elaborate injunctions against troubling to answer it.

Robert Drummond was an excellent and Christian man, but he had never been remarkable for profuse expenditure. In fact, he guarded his bawbees very carefully indeed, and among other judicious precautions he never sent telegrams if he could help it, and when fate forced his hand, kept very rigorously within the twelve-word limit. His telegrams in consequence were celebrated more for their conciseness than their clarity. Yet here he was sending a telegram thirty-four words long, apart from the address and signature, and spending halfpenny after halfpenny with reckless profusion to make every detail explicit!

Particularly curious were the three clauses all devoted to saving Mr Burnett the trouble of replying. Never before had Mr Drummond shown such extraordinary consideration for a friend's purse, and it is a discouraging feature of human nature that even the worthy Mr Burnett felt more puzzled than touched by his generous thoughtfulness.

"Robert Drummond never wrote out that wire himself," he concluded. "He must just have told some one what he wanted to say, and they must have written it themselves. Well, we'll hope they paid for it too, or Robert will be terrible annoyed."

The afternoon wore on, and as six o'clock drew near, the minister began to look out for Mr Taylor and his car. But six o'clock passed, and quarter-past six, and still there was no sign of him. The minister began to grow a little worried lest they should have to do most of the journey in the dark, for he was an inexperienced motorist, and such a long drive by night seemed to him a formidable and risky undertaking.

At last at half-past six the thrum of a car was heard, and a few minutes later a long, raking, dark-green touring car dashed up to the door of the modest manse. The minister hurried out to welcome his guest, and then stopped dead short in sheer astonishment. Mr Taylor was none other than the Lancashire lad.

On his part, Mr Taylor seemed almost equally surprised.

"Well, I'm blowed!" he cried jovially. "If this isn't the most extraordinary coincidence! When I got Robert Drummond's note, and noticed the part of the country you lived in, I wondered if you could possibly be the same minister I'd met; but it really seemed too good to be true! Delighted to meet you again!"

He laughed loud and cheerfully, and wrung the minister's hand like an old friend. Mr Burnett, though less demonstrative, felt heartily pleased, and led his guest cordially into the manse parlour.

"You'll have some tea before you start, I hope?" he inquired.

"Ra-ther!" cried Mr Taylor. "I've a Lancashire appetite for tea! Ha, ha, ha!"

"Well, I'll have it in at once," said the minister, ringing the bell, "for I suppose we ought not to postpone our start too long."

"No hurry at all, my dear fellow," said Mr Taylor, throwing himself into the easiest chair the minister possessed. "I mean to have a jolly good tuck in before I start!"

At that moment Mr Burnett remembered that this time he had seen a chauffeur in the car. He went hospitably out of the room and turned towards the front door. But hardly had he turned in that direction when he heard Mr Taylor call out –

"Hallo! Where are you going?"

And the next moment he was after the minister and had him by the arm just as they reached the open front door. Mr Burnett ever afterwards remembered the curious impression produced on him by the note in Mr Taylor's voice, and that hurried grip of the arm. Suspicion, alarm, a note of anger, all seemed to be blended.

"I – I was only going to ask your driver to come and have a cup of tea in the kitchen," stammered the embarrassed minister.

"My dear sir, he doesn't want any; I've asked him already!" said Mr Taylor. "I assure you honestly I have!"

Mr Burnett suffered himself to be led back wondering greatly. He had caught a glimpse of the chauffeur, a clean-shaven, well-turned-out man, sitting back in his seat with his cap far over his eyes, and even in that hurried glance at part of his face he had been struck with something curiously familiar about the man; though whether he had seen him before, or, if not, who he reminded him of, he was quite unable to say. And then there was Mr Taylor's extraordinary change of manner the very moment he started to see the chauffeur. He could make nothing of it at all, but for some little time afterwards he had a vague sense of disquiet.

Mr Taylor, on his part, had recovered his cheerfulness as quickly as he had lost it.

"Forgive me, my dear Mr Burnett," he said earnestly, yet always with the rich jolly note in his voice. "I must have seemed a perfect maniac. The truth is, between ourselves, I had a terrible suspicion you were going to offer my good James whisky!"

"Oh," said the minister. "Is he then – er – an abstainer?" Mr Taylor laughed pleasantly.

"I wish he were! A wee drappie is his one failing; ha, ha! I never allow my chauffeur to touch a drop while I'm on the road, Mr Burnett – never, sir!"

Mr Burnett was slow to suspect ill of anyone, but he was just as slow in getting rid of a suspicion. With all his simplicity, he could not but think that Mr Taylor jumped extraordinarily quickly to conclusions and got excited on smaller provocation than anyone he had ever met. Over his first cup of tea he sat very silent.

In the meantime the sociable Mary had been suffering from a sense of disappointment. Surely the beautiful liveried figure in the car would require his tea and eggs like his master? For a little she sat awaiting his arrival in the kitchen, with her cap neatly arranged, and an expectant smile. But gradually disappointment deepened. She considered the matter judicially. Clearly, she decided, Mr Burnett had forgotten the tradition of hospitality associated with that and every other manse. And then she decided that her own duty was plain.

She went out of the back door and round the house. There stood the car, with the resplendent figure leaning back in his seat, his cap still over his eyes, and his face now resting on his hand, so that she could barely see more than the tip of his nose. He heard nothing of her approach till she was fairly at his side, and in her high and penetrating voice cried –

"Will ye not be for a cup of tea and an egg to it, eh?" The chauffeur started, and Mary started too. She had seen his face for an instant, though he covered it quickly, but apparently quite naturally, with his hand.

"No, thanks," he said brusquely, and turned away his eyes.

Mary went back to the kitchen divided between annoyance at the rebuff and wonder. The liveried figure might have been the twin-brother of the minister.

III. – ON THE CLIFF.

GRADUALLY Mr Burnett recovered his composure. His guest was so genial and friendly and appreciative of the scones and the currant cake that he began to upbraid himself for churlishness in allowing anything like a suspicion of this pleasant gentleman to linger in his mind. There remained a persistent little shadow which he could not quite drive away, but he conscientiously tried his best. As for Mr Taylor, there never was a jollier and yet a more thoughtful companion.

He seemed to think of every mortal thing that the minister could possibly need for his journey.

"Got your passport?" he inquired.

"Yes," said the minister. "I am carrying it in my breast-pocket. It ought to be safe there."

"The safest place possible!" said Mr Taylor cordially. "It's all in order, I presume, eh?"

Mr Burnett took the passport out of his pocket and showed it to him. His guest closely examined the minister's photograph which was attached, went through all the particulars carefully, and pronounced everything in order, as far as an ignorant outsider like himself could judge.

"Of course," he said, "I'm a business man, Mr Burnett, and I can tell when a thing looks businesslike, though I know no more about what the authorities require and why they ask for all these particulars than you do. It's all red tape, I suppose."

As a further precaution he recommended his host to slip a few letters and a receipted bill or two into his pocket-book, so that he would have a ready means of establishing his identity if any difficulty arose. Mr Burnett was somewhat surprised, but accepted his guest's word for it, as a shrewd Lancashire lad, that these little tips were well worth taking.

By this time the evening was falling, and at length Mr Taylor declared himself ready for the road. He had drunk four cups of tea, and hurried over none of them. For a moment Mr Burnett half wondered if he had any reason for delaying their start, but immediately reproached himself for harbouring such a thought. Indeed, why should he think so? There seemed nothing whatever to be gained by delay, with the dusk falling so fast and a long road ahead.

The minister's rug and umbrella and two leather bags were put into the car, he and Mr Taylor got aboard, and off they went at last. Mr Burnett had another glance at the chauffeur, and again was haunted by an odd sense of familiarity; but once they had started, the view of his back in the gathering dusk suggested nothing more explicit.

Presently they passed a corner, and the minister looked round uneasily. "What road are you taking?" he asked.

"We're going to join the coast road from Berwick," said Mr Taylor.

"Isn't that rather roundabout?" Mr Taylor laughed jovially.

"My good James has his own ideas," said he. "As a matter of fact, I fancy he knows the coast road and isn't sure of the other. However, we needn't worry about that. With a car like this the difference in time will be a flea-bite!"

He had provided the minister with another excellent cigar, and smoking in comfort behind a glass wind-screen, with the dim country slipping by and the first pale star faintly shining overhead, the pair fell into easy discourse. Mr Taylor was a remarkably sympathetic talker, the minister found. He kept the conversation entirely on his companion's affairs, putting innumerable questions as to his habits and way of life, and indeed his whole history, and exhibiting a flattering interest in his answers. Mr Burnett said to himself at last, with a smile, that this inquiring gentleman would soon know as much about him as he knew himself.

Once or twice the minister wondered how fast they were really going. They did not seem to him to be achieving any very extraordinary speed, but possibly that was only because the big car ran so easily. In fact, when he once questioned his companion, Mr Taylor assured him that actually was the explanation. It was thus pretty dark when they struck the coast road, and it grew ever darker as they ran northward through a bare, treeless country, with the cliff edge never far away and the North Sea glimmering beyond.

They had reached an absolutely lonely stretch of road that hugged the shore closely when the car suddenly stopped. "Hallo!" exclaimed Mr Taylor, "what's up?"

The chauffeur half-turned round and said in a low voice "Did you see that light, sir?"

"Which light?"

The chauffeur pointed to the dark stretch of turf between them and the edge of the cliffs.

"Just there, sir. I saw it flash for a second. I got a glimpse of someone moving too, sir."

Mr Taylor became intensely excited. "A spy signalling!" he exclaimed.

"Looks like it, sir," said the chauffeur.

Mr Taylor turned to the minister with an eager, resolute air.

"Our duty's clear, Mr Burnett," said he. "As loyal subjects of King George – God bless him! – we've got to have a look into this!"

With that he jumped out and stood by the open door, evidently expecting the minister to follow. For a moment Mr Burnett hesitated. A vague sense that all was not well suddenly affected him. "Do not go!" something seemed to say to him. And yet as a man and a loyal subject how could he possibly decline to assist in an effort to foil the King's enemies? Reluctantly he descended from the car, and once he was on the road, Mr Taylor gave him no time for further debate.

"Come on!" he whispered eagerly; and then turning to the chauffeur, "come along too, James!"

Close by there was a gate in the fence, and they all three went through this and quietly crossed the short stretch of grass between the road and the cliffs, Mr Taylor and the minister walking in front and the chauffeur following close at their heels. Now that the car was silent, they could hear the soft lapping of the water at the cliff foot, but that and the fall of their feet on the short crisp turf were the only sounds.

Mr Burnett peered hard into the darkness, but he could see absolutely nothing. All at once he realised that they were getting very close to the brink, and that if there were anyone in front they would certainly be silhouetted against the sky. There could not possibly be any use in going further; why then did they continue to advance? At that a clear and terrifying instinct of danger seized him. He turned round sharply, and uttered one loud ringing cry.

He was looking straight into the chauffeur's face, and it seemed as though he were looking into his own, distorted by murderous intention. Above it the man's hand was already raised. It descended, and the minister fell on the turf with a gasp. He knew no more of that night's adventure.

IV. – MR DRUMMOND'S VISITOR.

UPON a secluded road in the quiet suburb of Trinity stood the residence of Mr Robert Drummond. It was a neat unpretentious little villa graced by a number of trees and a clinging Virginia creeper, and Mr Drummond was a neat unpretentious little gentleman, graced by a number of virtues, and a devoted Mrs Drummond. From the upper windows of his house you could catch a glimpse of the castled and templed hills of Edinburgh on the one side, and the shining Forth and green coasts of Fife on the other. The Forth, in fact, was close at hand, and of late Mr Drummond had been greatly entertained by observing many interesting movements upon its waters.

He had looked forward to exhibiting and expounding these features to his friend Mr Burnett, and felt considerably disappointed when upon the morning of the day when the minister should have come, a telegram arrived instead. It ran –

"Unavoidably prevented from coming to stay with you. Shall explain later. Many regrets. Don't trouble reply. Leaving home immediately.

"BURNETT."

As Mr Drummond studied this telegram he began to feel not only disappointed but a trifle critical.

"Alec Burnett must have come into a fortune!" he said to himself. "Six words – the whole of threepence – wasted in telling me not to reply! As if I'd be spending my money on anything so foolish. I never saw such extravagance!"

On the following morning Mr Drummond was as usual up betimes. He had retired a year or two before from a responsible position in an insurance office, but he still retained his active business habits, and by eight o'clock every morning of the summer was out and busy in his garden. It still wanted ten minutes to eight, and he was just buttoning up his waistcoat when he heard the front-door bell ring. A minute or two later the maid announced that Mr Topham was desirous of seeing Mr Drummond immediately.

"Mr Topham?" he asked.

"He's a Navy Officer, sir," said the maid.

Vaguely perturbed, Mr Drummond hurried downstairs, and found in his study a purposeful-looking young man, with the two zigzag stripes on his sleeve of a lieutenant in the Royal Naval Reserve.

"Mr Drummond?" he inquired.

"The same," said Mr Drummond, firmly yet cautiously.

"You expected a visit from a Mr Burnett yesterday, I believe?"

"I had been expecting him till I got his wire."

"His wire!" exclaimed Lieutenant Topham. "Did he telegraph to you?"

"Yes: he said he couldn't come."

"May I see that telegram?"

Caution had always been Mr Drummond's most valuable asset.

"Is it important?" he inquired.

"Extremely," said the lieutenant a trifle brusquely.

Mr Drummond went to his desk and handed him the telegram. He could see Topham's eyebrows rise as he read it.

"Thank you," he said when he had finished. "May I keep it?"

Without waiting for permission, he put it in his pocket, and with a grave air said –

"I am afraid I have rather serious news to give you about Mr Burnett."

"Dear me!" cried Mr Drummond. "It's not mental trouble, I hope? That was a queer wire he sent me!"

"He didn't send you that wire," said Lieutenant Topham.

"What!" exclaimed Mr Drummond. "Really – you don't say so? Then who did?"

"That's what we've got to find out."

The lieutenant glanced at the door, and added –

"I think we had better come a little farther away from the door."

They moved to the farther end of the room and sat down. "Mr Burnett has been knocked on the head and then nearly drowned," said the lieutenant.

Mr Drummond cried aloud in horror. Topham made a warning gesture.

"This is not to be talked about at present," he said in a guarded voice. "The facts simply are that I'm in command of a patrol-boat, and last night we were off the Berwickshire coast when we found your friend in the water with a bad wound in his head and a piece of cord tied round his feet."

" You mean someone had tried to murder him?" cried Mr Drummond.

"It looked rather like it," said Topham drily.

"And him a minister too!" gasped Mr Drummond.

"So we found later."

"But you'd surely tell that from his clothes!"

"He had no clothes when we found him."

"No clothes on! Then do you mean —"

"We took him straight back to the base," continued the lieutenant quickly, "and finally he came round and was able to talk a little. Then we learned his name and heard of you, and Captain Blacklock asked me to run up and let you know he was safe, and also get you to check one or two of his statements. Mr Burnett is naturally a little light-headed at present."

Mr Drummond was a persistent gentleman.

"But do you mean you found him with no clothes on right out at sea?"

"No; close under the cliffs."

"Did you see him fall into the water?"

"We heard a cry, and picked him up shortly afterwards," said the lieutenant, rather evasively, Mr Drummond thought. "However, the main thing is that he will recover all right. You can rest assured he is being well looked after."

"I'd like to know more about this," said Mr Drummond with an air of determination.

"So would we," said Topham drily, "and I'd just like to ask you one or two questions, if I may. Mr Burnett was on his way to the Windy Islands, I believe?"

"He was. He had got all his papers and everything ready to start to-night."

"You feel sure of that?"

"He wrote and told me so himself."

Lieutenant Topham nodded in silence. Then he inquired—

"Do you know a Mr Taylor?"

"Taylor? I know a John Taylor—"

"Who comes from Lancashire and keeps a motor-car?"

"No," said Mr Drummond. "I don't know that one. Why?"

"Then you didn't send a long telegram to Mr Burnett yesterday telling him that Mr Taylor would call for him in his motor-car and drive him to your house?"

"Certainly not!" cried Mr Drummond indignantly. "I never sent a long telegram to any one in my life. I tell you I don't know anything about this Mr Taylor or his motor-car. If Mr Burnett told you that, he's light-headed indeed!"

"Those are merely the questions Captain Blacklock asked me to put," said the lieutenant soothingly.

"Is he the officer in command of the base?" demanded Mr Drummond a little fiercely.

"No," said Topham briefly; "Commander Blacklock is an officer on special service at present."

"Commander!" exclaimed Mr Drummond with a menacing sniff. "But you just called him Captain."

"Commanders get the courtesy title of Captain," explained the lieutenant, rising as he spoke. "Thank you very much, Mr Drummond. There's only one thing more I'd like to say—"

"Ay, but there are several things *I'd* like to say!" said Mr Drummond very firmly. "I want to know what's the meaning of this outrage to my friend. What's your theory?"

Before the war Lieutenant Topham had been an officer in a passenger liner, but he had already acquired in great perfection the real Navy mask.

"It seems rather mysterious," he replied – in a most unsuitably light and indifferent tone, Mr Drummond considered.

"But surely you have *some* ideas!" The Lieutenant shook his head.

"We'll probably get to the bottom of it sooner or later."

"A good deal later than sooner, I'm afraid," said Mr Drummond severely. "You've informed the police, I presume."

"The affair is not in my hands, Mr Drummond."

"Then whose hands is it in?"

"I have not been consulted on that point."

Ever since the war broke out Mr Drummond's views concerning the Navy had been in a state of painful flux. Sometimes he felt a genuine pride as a taxpayer in having provided himself with such an efficient and heroic service; at other times he sadly suspected that his money had been wasted, and used to urge upon all his acquaintance the strong opinion that the Navy should really "do something" – and be quick about it too!

Lieutenant Topham depressed him greatly. There seemed such an extraordinary lack of intelligent interest about the fellow. How differently Nelson would have replied!

"Well, there's one thing I absolutely insist upon getting at the bottom of," he said resolutely. "I am accused of sending a long telegram to Mr Burnett about a Mr Taylor. Now I want to know the meaning of that!"

Lieutenant Topham smiled, but his smile, instead of soothing, merely provoked the indignant householder.

"Neither you nor Mr Burnett are accused of sending telegrams. We only know that you received them."

"Then who sent them, I'd like to know?"

"That, no doubt, will appear in time. I must get back now, Mr Drummond; but I must first ask you not to mention a word to anyone of this – in the meantime anyhow."

The householder looked considerably taken aback. He had anticipated making a very pleasant sensation among his friends.

"I – er – of course shall use great discretion –" he began.

Lieutenant Topham shook his head.

"I am directed to ask you to tell *nobody*."

"Of course Mrs Drummond –"

"Not even Mrs Drummond."

"But this is really very high-handed, sir! Mr Burnett is a very old friend of mine –"

The Lieutenant came a step nearer to him, and said very earnestly and persuasively –

"You have an opportunity, Mr Drummond, of doing a service to your country by keeping absolute silence. We can trust you to do that for England, surely?"

"For Great Britain," corrected Mr Drummond, who was a member of a society for propagating bagpipe music and of another for commemorating Bannockburn, – "well, yes, if you put it like that – Oh, certainly, certainly. Yes, you can trust me, Mr Topham. But – er – what am I to say to Mrs Drummond about your visit?"

"Say that I was sent to ask you to keep your lights obscured," suggested the lieutenant with a smile.

"Capital!" said the householder. "I've warned her several times about the pantry window. That will kill two birds with one stone!"

"Good morning, sir. Thank you very much," said the lieutenant.

Mr Drummond was left in a very divided state of mind regarding the Navy's competence, Mr Burnett's sanity, and his own judgment.

V. – ON THE MAIL BOAT.

A PROCESSION came down the long slope at the head of the bay. Each vehicle but one rumbled behind a pair of leisurely horses. That one, a car with a passenger and his luggage, hooted from tail to head of the procession, and vanished in the dust towards the pier. The sea stretched like a sheet of brilliant glass right out across the bay and the firth beyond to the great blue island hills, calm as far as the eye could search it; on the green treeless shores, with their dusty roads and their dykes of flagstones set on edge, there was scarcely enough breeze to stir the grasses. "We shall have a fine crossing," said the passengers in the coaches to one another.

They bent round the corner of the bay and passed the little row of houses, pressed close beneath the high grassy bank, and rumbled on to the pier. The sentries and the naval guard eyed the passengers with professional suspicion as they gathered in a queue to show their passports, and then gradually straggled towards the mail boat. But there was one passenger who was particularly eyed; though if all the glances toward her were prompted by suspicion, it was well concealed. She was a girl of anything from twenty-two to twenty-five, lithe, dressed to a miracle, dark-haired, and more than merely pretty. Her dark eyebrows nearly meeting, her bright and singularly intelligent eyes, her firm mouth and resolute chin, the mixture of thoughtfulness in her expression and decision in her movements, were not the usual ingredients of prettiness. Yet her features were so fine and her complexion so clear, and there was so much charm as well as thought in her expression, that the whole effect of her was delightful. Undoubtedly she was beautiful.

She was clearly travelling alone, and evidently a stranger to those parts. No one on the pier or steamer touched a hat or greeted her, and from her quick looks of interest it was plain that everything was fresh to her. The string of passengers was blocked for a moment on the narrow deck, and just where she paused stood a tall man who had come aboard a minute or two before. He took his eyes discreetly off her face, and they fell upon her bag. There on the label he could plainly read, "Miss Eileen Holland." Then she passed on, and the tall man kept looking after her.

Having piled her lighter luggage on a seat in a very brisk and business-like fashion, Miss Holland strolled across the deck and leaned with her back against the railings and her hands in the pockets of her loose tweed coat, studying with a shrewd glance her fellow-passengers. They included a number of soldiers in khaki, on leave apparently; several nondescript and uninteresting people, mostly female; and the tall man. At him she glanced several times. He was very obviously a clergyman of some sort, in the conventional black felt hat and a long dark overcoat; and yet though his face was not at all unclerical, it seemed to her that he was not exactly the usual type. Then she saw his eyes turn on her again, and she gazed for some minutes at the pier just above their heads.

The cable was cast off and the little steamer backed through the foam of her own wake, and wheeling, set forth for the Isles. For a while Miss Holland watched the green semicircle slowly receding astern and the shining waters opening ahead, and then turned to a more practical matter. Other passengers were eyeing the laden deck-seat.

"I'm afraid my things are in your way," she said, and crossing the deck took up a bag and looked round where to put it.

The clergyman was beside her in a stride.

"Allow me. I'll stow it away for you," he said.

He spoke with a smile, but with an air of complete decision and quiet command, and with a murmur of thanks she yielded the bag almost automatically. As he moved off with it, it struck her that here was a clergyman apparently accustomed to very prompt obedience from his flock.

They had been standing just aft of the deck-house, and with the bag in his hand he passed by this to where a pile of lighter luggage had been arranged on the deck. As he went he looked at the bag curiously, and then before putting it down he glanced over his shoulder. The lady was not in sight, and very swiftly but keenly he studied it more closely. It was a suit-case made of an unusual brown, light material. Turning one end up quickly he read on a little plate this assurance by the makers, "Garantirt echt Vulcanfibre." And then slowly, and apparently rather thoughtfully, he strolled back.

"You'll find it among the other luggage, just beyond the deck-house," he said, and then with an air of sudden thought, added, "Perhaps I ought to have put it with your other things, wherever they are."

"I have practically nothing else," said she, "except a trunk in the hold."

"You are travelling very light," he remarked. "That wasn't a very substantial suit-case."

For a moment she seemed to be a little doubtful whether to consider him a somewhat forward stranger. Then she said with a frank smile –

"No; it was made in Germany."

As she spoke he glanced at her with a curious sudden intensity, that might have been an ordinary trick of manner.

"Oh," he said with a smile. "Before the war, I presume?"

"Yes," she answered briefly, and looked round her as though wondering whether she should move.

But the clergyman seemed oblivious to the hint.

"Do you know Germany well?" he asked.

"Yes." she said. "Do you?"

He nodded.

"Yes, pretty well – as it was before the war, of course. I had some good friends there at one time."

"So had I," she said.

"All in the past tense now," said he.

"I suppose so," she answered; "yet I sometimes find it hard to believe that they are all as poisoned against England and as ignorant and callous as people think. I can't picture some of my friends like that!"

She seemed to have got over her first touch of resentment. There was certainly an air of good-breeding and even of distinction about the man, and after all, his extreme assurance sat very naturally on him. It had an unpremeditated matter-of-course quality that made it difficult to remain offended.

"It is hard to picture a good many things," he said thoughtfully. "Were you long in Germany?"

She told him two years, and then questioned him in return; but he seemed to have a gift for conveying exceedingly little information with an air of remarkable finality – as though he had given a complete report and there was an end of it. On the other hand, he had an equal gift for putting questions in a way that made it impossible not to answer without churlishness. For his manner never lacked courtesy, and he showed a flattering interest in each word of her replies. She felt that she had never met a man who had put her more on her mettle and made her instinctively wish more to show herself to advantage.

Yet she seemed fully capable of holding her own, for after half an hour's conversation it would have been remarkably difficult to essay a biographical sketch of Miss Eileen Holland. She had spent a number of years abroad, and confessed to being a fair linguist; she was going to the Islands "to stay with some people"; and she had previously done "a little" war work – so little, apparently, that she had been advised to seek a change of air, as her companion observed with a smile.

"Anyhow, I have not done enough," she said with a sudden intensity of suppressed feeling in her voice.

The keen-faced clergyman glanced at her quickly, but said nothing. A minute or two later he announced that he had some correspondence to look over, and thereupon he left her with the same air of decision instantly acted on with which he had first addressed her. He passed through the door of the deck-house, and she got a glimpse of his head going down the companion. Her face remained quite composed, but in her eyes there seemed to be the trace of a suggestion that she was unused to see gentlemen quit her side quite so promptly.

A few minutes later she went down herself to the ladies' cabin. Coming out, the foot of the companion was immediately opposite, and beyond stretched the saloon. At the far end of this sat the clergyman, and at the sight of him Miss Holland paused for a moment at the foot of the ladder and looked at him with a face that seemed to show both a little amusement and a little wonder. He sat quite by himself, with a bundle of papers on the table at his elbow. One of these was in his hand, and he was reading it with an air of extraordinary concentration. He had carelessly pushed back his black felt hat, and what arrested her was the odd impression this produced. With his hat thus rakishly tilted, all traces of his clerical profession seemed mysteriously to have vanished. The white dog-collar was there all right, but unaided it seemed singularly incapable of making him into a conventional minister. Miss Holland went up on deck rather thoughtfully.

The little mail boat was now far out in the midst of a waste of waters. The ill-omened tideway was on its best behaviour; but even so, there was a constant gentle roll as the oily swell swung in from the Atlantic. Ahead, on the starboard bow, loomed the vast island precipices; astern the long Scottish coast faded into haze. One other vessel alone was to be seen – a long, low, black ship with a single spike of a mast and several squat funnels behind it. An eccentric vessel this seemed; for she first meandered towards the mail boat and then meandered away again, with no visible business on the waters.

The girl moved along the deck till she came to the place where her suit-case had been stowed. Close beside it were two leather kit-bags, and as she paused there it was on these that her eyes fell. She looked at them, in fact, very attentively. On each were the initials "A.B.", and on their labels the legend, "The Rev. Alex. Burnett." She came a step nearer and studied them still more closely. A few old luggage-labels were still affixed, and one at least of these bore the word "Berwick." Miss Holland seemed curiously interested by her observations.

A little later the clergyman reappeared, and approached her like an old acquaintance. By this time they were running close under the cliffs, and they gazed together up to the dizzy heights a thousand feet above their heads, where dots of sea-birds circled hardly to be distinguished by the eye, and then down to the green swell and bursting foam at the foot of that stupendous wall. In the afternoon sun it glowed like a wall of copper. For a few minutes both were instinctively silent. There was nothing to be said of such a spectacle.

Then Miss Holland suddenly asked:

"Do you live near the sea?"

"Not very," he answered with his air of finality. But this time she persisted.

"What is your part of the country?" "Berwickshire," he said briefly.

"Do you happen to know a minister there – a Mr Burnett?" she inquired.

"That is my own name," he said quietly. "Mr Alexander Burnett?"

He nodded.

"That is very funny," she said. "There must be two of you. I happen to have stayed in those parts and met the other."

There seemed to be no expression at all in his eyes as they met hers; nor did hers reveal anything. Then he looked round them quietly. There were several passengers not far away.

"It would be rather pleasant in the bows," he suggested. "Shall we move along there for a little?"

He made the proposal very courteously, and yet it sounded almost as much a command as a suggestion, and he began to move even as he spoke. She started too, and exchanging a casual sentence as they went, they made their way forward till they stood together in the very prow with the bow wave beneath their feet, and the air beating cold upon their faces, – a striking solitary couple.

"I'm wondering if yon's a married meenister!" said one of their fellow-passengers – a facetious gentleman. "It's no' his wife, anyhow!" grinned his friend. A little later the wit wondered again.

"I'm wondering how long thae two are gaun tae stand there!" he said this time.

The cliffs fell and a green sound opened. The mail boat turned into the sound, opening inland prospects all the while. A snug bay followed the sound, with a little grey-gabled town clinging to the very wash of the tide, and a host of little vessels in the midst. Into the bay pounded the mail boat and up towards the town, and only then did the gallant minister and his fair acquaintance stroll back from the bows. The wag and his friend looked at them curiously, but they had to admit that such a prolonged flirtation had seldom left fewer visible traces. They might have been brother and sister, they both looked so indifferent.

The gangway shot aboard, and with a brief hand-shake the pair parted. A few minutes later Miss Holland was being greeted by an elderly gentleman in a heavy ulster, whilst the minister was following a porter towards a small waggonette.

VI. – THE VANISHING GOVERNESS.

THE house of Breck was a mansion of tolerable antiquity as mansions went in the islands, and several curious stories had already had time to encrust it, like lichen on an aged wall. But none of them were stranger than the quite up-to-date and literally true story of the vanishing governess.

Richard Craigie, Esq., of Breck, the popular, and more or less respected, laird of the mansion and estate, was a stout, grey-bearded gentleman, with a twinkling blue eye, and one of the easiest-going dispositions probably in Europe. His wife, the respected, and more or less popular, mistress of the mansion, was lean and short, and very energetic. Their sons were employed at present like everybody else's sons, and do not concern this narrative. But their two daughters, aged fifteen and fourteen, were at home, and do concern it materially.

It was only towards the end of July that Mrs. Craigie thought of having a governess for the two girls during the summer holidays. With a letter in her hand, she bustled into Mr Craigie's smoking-room, and announced that her friend Mrs Armitage, in Kensington, knew a lady who knew a charming and well-educated girl –

"And who does she know?" interrupted her husband. "Nobody," said Mrs Craigie. "She *is* the girl!"

"Oh!" said the laird. "Now I thought that she would surely know another girl who knows a woman, who knows a man –"

"Richard!" said his wife. "Kindly listen to me!"

It had been her fate to marry a confirmed domestic humorist, but she bore her burden stoically. She told him now simply and firmly that the girl in question required a holiday, and that she proposed to give her one, and in return extract some teaching and supervision for their daughters.

"Have it your own way, my dear. Have it your own way," said he. "It was economy yesterday. It's a governess today. Have you forced the safe?"

"Which safe?" demanded the unsuspecting lady.

"At the bank. I've no more money of my own, I can tell you. However, send for your governess – get a couple of them as you're at it!"

The humorist was clearly so pleased with his jest that no further debate was to be apprehended, and his wife went out to write the letter. Mr Craigie lit his sixteenth pipe since breakfast and chewed the cud of his wit very happily.

A fortnight later he returned one evening in the car, bringing Miss Eileen Holland, with her trunk and her brown suit-case.

"My hat, Selina!" said he to his wife, as soon as the girls had led Miss Holland out of hearing, "that's the kind of governess for me! You don't mind my telling her to call me Dick, do you? It slipped out when she was squeezing my hand."

"I don't mind you're being undignified," replied Mrs Craigie in a chilly voice, "but I do wish you wouldn't be vulgar."

As Mr Craigie's chief joys in life were entertaining his daughters and getting a rise out of his wife, and as he also had a very genuine admiration for a pretty face, he was in the seventh heaven of happiness, and remained there for the next three days. Pipe in mouth, he invaded the schoolroom constantly and unseasonably, and reduced his daughters to a state of incoherent giggling by retailing to Miss Holland various ingenious schemes for their corporal punishment, airing humorous fragments of a language he called French, and questioning their instructor on suppositious romantic episodes in her career. He thought Miss Holland hardly laughed as much as she ought; still, she was a fine girl.

At table he kept his wife continually scandalised by his jocularities; such as hoarsely whispering, "I've lost my half of the sixpence, Miss Holland," or repeating, with a thoughtful air, "Under the apple tree when the moon rises – I must try and not forget the hour!" Miss Holland was even less responsive to these sallies, but he enjoyed them enormously himself, and still maintained she was a fine girl.

Mrs Craigie's opinion of her new acquisition was only freely expressed afterwards, and then she declared that clever though Miss Holland undoubtedly was, and superior though she seemed, she had always suspected that something was a little wrong somewhere. She and Mr Craigie had used considerable influence and persuasion to obtain a passport for her, and why should they have been called upon to do this (by a lady whom Mrs Armitage admitted she had only met twice), simply to give a change of air to a healthy-looking girl? There was something behind *that*. Besides, Miss Holland was just a trifle too good-looking. That type always had a history.

"My wife was plain Mrs Craigie before the thing happened," observed her husband with a twinkle, "but, dash it, she's been Mrs Solomon ever since!"

It was on the fourth morning of Miss Holland's visit that the telegram came for her. Mr Craigie himself brought it into the schoolroom and delivered it with much facetious mystery. He noticed that it seemed to contain a message of some importance, and that she failed to laugh at all when he offered waggishly to put 'him' up for the night. But she simply put it in her pocket and volunteered no explanation. He went away feeling that he had wasted a happy quip.

After lunch Mrs Craigie and the girls were going out in the car, and Miss Holland was to have accompanied them. It was then that she made her only reference to the telegram. She had got a wire, she said, and had a long letter to write, and so begged to be excused. Accordingly the car went off without her.

Not five minutes later Mr Craigie was smoking a pipe and trying to summon up energy to go for a stroll, when Miss Holland entered the smoking-room. He noticed that she had never looked so smiling and charming.

"Oh, Mr Craigie," she said, " I want you to help me. I'm preparing a little surprise!"

"For the girls?"

"For all of you!"

The laird loved a practical jest, and scented happiness at once.

"I'm your man!" said he. "What can I do for you?"

"I'll come down again in half an hour," said she. "And then I want you to help me to carry something."

She gave him a swift bewitching smile that left him entirely helpless, and hurried from the room.

Mr Craigie looked at the clock and decided that he would get his stroll into the half-hour, so he took his stick and sauntered down the drive. On one side of this drive was a line of huddled wind-bent trees, and at the end was a gate opening on the highroad, with the sea close at hand. Just as he got to the gate a stranger appeared upon the road, walking very slowly, and up to that moment concealed by the trees. He was a clergyman, tall, clean-shaved, and with what the laird afterwards described as a "hawky kind of look."

There was no haughtiness whatever about the laird of Breck. He accosted everyone he met, and always in the friendliest way.

"A fine day!" said he heartily. "Grand weather for the crops, if we could just get a wee bit more of rain soon."

The clergyman stopped.

"Yes, sir," said he, "it is fine weather."

His manner was polite, but not very hearty, the laird thought. However, he was not easily damped, and proceeded to contribute several more observations, chiefly regarding the weather prospects, and tending to become rapidly humorous And then he remembered his appointment in the smoking room.

"Well," said he, "good day to you! I must be moving I'm afraid."

"Good day," said the stranger courteously, and moved off promptly as he spoke.

"I wonder who will that minister be?" said Mr Craigie to himself as he strolled back. "It's funny I never saw the man before. And I wonder, too, where he was going?" And then it occurred to him as an odd circumstance that the minister had started to go back again, not to continue as he had been walking.

"That's a funny thing," he thought.

He had hardly got back to his smoking-room when Miss Holland appeared, dressed to go out, in hat and tweed coat, and dragging, of all things, her brown suit-case. It seemed to be heavily laden.

She smiled at him confidentially, as one fellow-conspirator at another.

"Do you mind giving me a hand with this?" said she.

"Hullo!" cried the laird. "What's this – an elopement? Can you not wait till I pack my things too? The minister's in no hurry. I've just been speaking to him."

It struck him that Miss Holland took his jest rather seriously.

"The minister?" said she in rather an odd voice. "You've spoken to him?"

"He was only asking if I had got the licence," winked Mr Craigie.

The curious look passed from her face, and she laughed as pleasantly as he could wish.

"I'll take the bag myself," said the laird. "Oh, it's no weight for me. I used to be rather a dab at throwing the hammer in my day. But where am I to take it?"

"I'll show you," said she.

So out they set, Mr Craigie carrying the suit-case, and Miss Holland in the most delightful humour beside him. He felt he could have carried it for a very long way. She led him through the garden and out into a side lane between the wall and a hedge.

"Just put it down here," she said. "And now I want you to come back for something else, if you don't mind."

"Mind?" said the laird gallantly. "Not me! But I'm wondering what you are driving at."

She only smiled, but from her merry eye he felt sure that some very brilliant jest was afoot, and he joked away pleasantly as they returned to the house.

"Now," she said, "do you mind waiting in the smoking-room for ten minutes or so?"

She went out, and Mr Craigie waited, mystified but happy.

He waited for ten minutes; he waited for twenty, he waited for half an hour, and still there was no sign of the fascinating Miss Holland. And then he sent a servant to look for her. Her report gave Mr Craigie the strongest sensation that had stirred that good-natured humorist for many a day. Miss Holland was not in her room, and no more, apparently, were her belongings. The toilette table was stripped, the wardrobe was empty; in fact, the only sign of her was her trunk, strapped and locked.

Moving with exceptional velocity, Mr Craigie made straight for the lane beyond the garden. The brown suit-case had disappeared.

"Well, I'm jiggered!" murmured the baffled humorist. Very slowly and soberly he returned to the house, lit a fresh pipe, and steadied his nerves with a glass of grog. When Mrs Craigie returned, she found him sufficiently revived to jest again, though in a minor key.

"To think of the girl having the impudence to make me carry her luggage out of the house for her!" said he. "Gad, but it was a clever dodge to get clear with no one suspecting her! Well, anyhow, my reputation is safe again at last, Selina."

"Your reputation!" replied Mrs Craigie in a withering voice. "For what? Not for common-sense anyhow!"

"You're flustered, my dear," said the laird easily. "It's a habit women get into terrible easy. You should learn a lesson from Miss Eileen Holland. Dashed if I ever met a cooler hand in *my* life!"

"And what do you mean to do about it?" demanded his wife. "Do?" asked Mr Craigie, mildly surprised. "Well, we might leave the pantry window open at night, so that she can get in again if she's wanting to; or –"

"It's your duty to inform the authorities, Richard!"

"Duty?" repeated the laird, still more surprised. "Fancy me starting to do my duty at my time of life!"

"Anyhow," cried Mrs Craigie, "we've still got her trunk!"

"Ah," said Mr Craigie, happily at last, "so we have! Well, that's all right then."

And with a benign expression the philosopher contentedly lit another pipe.

PART III.

LIEUTENANT VON BELKE'S NARRATIVE RESUMED.

I. – THE MEETING.

AS the dusk rapidly thickened and I lay in the heather waiting for the signal, I gave myself one last bit of good advice. Of 'him' I was to meet, I had received officially a pretty accurate description, and unofficially heard one or two curious stories. I had also, of course, had my exact relationship to him officially defined. I was to be under his orders, generally speaking; but in purely naval matters, or at least on matters of naval detail, my judgment would be accepted by him. My last word of advice to myself simply was to be perfectly firm on any such point, and permit no scheme to be set afoot, however tempting, unless it was thoroughly practical from the naval point of view.

From the rim of my hollow there on the hillside I could see several of the farms below me, as well as the manse, and I noted one little sign of British efficiency – no glimmer of light shown from any of their windows. At sea a light or two twinkled intermittently, and a searchlight was playing, though fortunately not in my direction. Otherwise land and water were alike plunged in darkness. And then at last one single window of the manse glowed red for an instant. A few seconds passed, and it shone red again. Finally it showed a brighter yellow light twice in swift succession.

I rose and very carefully led my cycle over the heather down to the road, and then, still pushing it, walked quickly down the steep hill to where the side road turned off. There was not a sound save my footfall as I approached the house. A dark mass loomed in front of me, which I saw in a moment to be a garden wall with a few of the low wind-bent island trees showing above it. This side road led right up to an iron gate in the wall, and just as I got close enough to distinguish the bars, I heard a gentle creak and saw them begin to swing open. Beyond, the trees overarched the drive, and the darkness was profound. I had passed between the gate-posts before I saw or heard anything more. And then a quiet voice spoke.

"It is a dark night," it said in perfect English.

"Dark as pitch," I answered.

"It was darker last night," said the voice.

"It is dark enough," I answered.

Not perhaps a very remarkable conversation, you may think; but I can assure you my fingers were on my revolver, just in case one single word had been different. Now I breathed freely at last.

"Herr Tiel?" I inquired.

"Mr Tiel," corrected the invisible man beside me.

I saw him then for the first time as he stepped out from the shelter of the trees and closed the gate behind me-a tall dim figure in black.

"I'll lead your cycle," he said in a low voice, as he came back to me; "I know the way best."

He took it from me, and as we walked side by side towards the house he said–

"Permit me, Mr Belke, to give you one little word of caution. While you are here, forget that you can talk German! *Think* in English, if you can. We are walking on a tight-rope, not on the pavement. *No* precaution is excessive!"

"I understand," I said briefly.

There was in his voice, perfectly courteous though it was, a note of command which made one instinctively reply briefly – and obediently. I felt disposed to be favourably impressed with my ally.

He left me standing for a moment in the drive while he led my motor-cycle round to some shed at the back, and then we entered the house by the front door.

"My servant doesn't spend the night here," he explained, "so we are safe enough after dark, as long as we make no sound that can be heard outside."

It was pitch-dark inside, and only when he had closed and bolted the front door behind us, did Tiel flash his electric torch. Then I saw that we stood in a small porch which opened into a little hall, with a staircase facing us and a passage opening beside it into the back of the house. At either side was a door, and Tiel opened that on the right and led me into a pleasant, low, lamp-lit room with a bright peat fire blazing and a table laid for supper. I learned afterwards that the clergyman who had just vacated the parish had left hurriedly, and that his books and furniture had not yet followed him. Hence the room, and indeed the whole house, looked habitable and comfortable.

"This is the place I have been looking for for a long time!" I cried cheerfully, for indeed it made a pleasant contrast to a ruinous farm or the interior of a submarine.

Tiel smiled. He had a pleasant smile, but it generally passed from his face very swiftly, and left his expression cool, alert, composed, and a trifle dominating.

"You had better take off your overalls and begin," he said. "There is an English warning against conversation between a full man and a fasting. I have had supper already."

When I took off my overalls, I noticed that he gave me a quick look of surprise.

"In uniform!" he exclaimed.

"It may not be much use if I'm caught," I laughed, "but I thought it a precaution worth taking."

"Excellent!" he agreed, and he seemed genuinely pleased. "It was very well thought of. Do you drink whisky-and-soda?"

"You have no beer?"

He smiled and shook his head.

"I am a Scottish divine," he said, "and I am afraid my guests must submit to whisky. Even in these little details it is well to be correct."

For the next half-hour there was little conversation. To tell you the truth I was nearly famished, and had something better to do than talk. Tiel on his part opened a newspaper, and now and then read extracts aloud. It was an English newspaper, of course, and I laughed once or twice at its items. He smiled too, but he did not seem much given to laughter. And all the while I took stock of my new acquaintance very carefully.

In appearance Adolph Tiel was just as he had been described to me, and very much as my imagination had filled in the picture: a man tall, though not very tall, clean-shaved, rather thin, decidedly English in his general aspect, distinctly good-looking, with hair beginning to turn grey, and cleverness marked clearly in his face. What I had not been quite prepared for was his air of good-breeding and authority. Not that there was any real reason why these qualities should have been absent, but as a naval officer of a country whose military services have pretty strong prejudices, I had scarcely expected to find in a secret-service agent quite this air.

Also what I had heard of Tiel had prepared me to meet a gentleman in whom cleverness was more conspicuous than dignity. Even those who professed to know something about him had admitted that he was a bit of a mystery. He was said to come either from Alsace or Lorraine, and to be of mixed parentage and the most cosmopolitan experience. One story had it that he served at one period of his very diverse career in the navy of a certain South American State, and this story I very soon came to the conclusion was correct, for he showed a considerable knowledge of naval affairs. Even when he professed ignorance of certain points, I was inclined to suspect he was simply trying to throw doubt upon the reports which he supposed I had heard, for rumour also said that he had quitted the service of his adopted country under circumstances which reflected more credit on his brains than his honesty.

In fact, my informants were agreed that Herr Tiel's brains were very remarkable indeed, and that his nerve and address were equal to his ability. He was undoubtedly very completely in the confidence of my own Government, and I could mention at least two rather serious mishaps that had befallen England which were credited to him by people who certainly ought to have known the facts.

Looking at him attentively as he sat before the fire studying 'The Scotsman' (the latest paper to be obtained in those parts), I thought to myself that here was a man I should a very great deal sooner have on my side than against me. If ever I had seen a wolf in sheep's clothing, it seemed to me that I beheld one now in the person of Adolph Tiel, attired as a Scottish clergyman, reading a solid Scottish newspaper over the peat fire of this remote and peaceful manse. And, to complete the picture, there sat I arrayed in a German naval uniform, with the unsuspecting Grand Fleet on the other side of those shuttered and curtained windows. The piquancy of the whole situation struck me so forcibly that I laughed aloud.

Tiel looked up and laid down his paper, and his eyebrows rose inquiringly. He was not a man who wasted many words.

"We are a nice pair!" I exclaimed.

I seemed to read approval of my spirit in his eye.

"You seem none the worse of your adventures," he said with a smile.

"No thanks to you!" I laughed.

Again he gave me that keen look of inquiry.

"I landed on this infernal island last night!" I explained.

"The deuce you did!" said he. "I was afraid you might, but as things turned out I couldn't get here sooner. What did you do with yourself?"

"First give me one of those cigars," I said, "and then I'll tell you."

He handed me the box of cigars and I drew up an easychair on the other side of the fire. And then I told him my adventures, and as I was not unwilling that this redoubtable adventurer should see that he had a not wholly unworthy accomplice, I told them in pretty full detail. He was an excellent listener, I must say that for him. With an amused yet appreciative smile, putting in now and then a question shrewd and to the point, he heard my tale to the end. And then he said in a quiet manner which I already realised detracted nothing from the value of his approval –

"You did remarkably well, Mr Belke. I congratulate you."

"Thank you, Mr Tiel," I replied. "And now may I ask you your adventures?"

"Certainly," said he. "I owe you an explanation."

II. – TIEL'S STORY.

"How much do you know of our scheme?" asked Tiel.

I shrugged my shoulders.

"Merely that you were going to impersonate a clergyman who was due to come here and preach this next Sunday. How you were going to achieve this feat I wasn't told."

He leaned back in his chair and sucked at his pipe, and then he began his story with a curious detached air, as though he were surveying his own handiwork from the point of view of an impartial connoisseur.

"The idea was distinctly ingenious," said he, "and I think I may also venture to claim for it a little originality. I won't trouble you with the machinery by which we learn things. It's enough to mention that among the little things we did learn was the fact that the minister of this parish had left for another charge, and that the parishioners were choosing his successor after the Scottish custom – by hearing a number of candidates each preach a trial sermon." He broke off and asked,

"Do you happen to have heard of Schumann?"

"You don't mean the great Schumann?"

"I mean a certain gentleman engaged in the same quiet line of business as myself. He is known of course under another name in England, where he is considered a very fine specimen of John Bull at his best – a jovial, talkative, commercial gentleman with nice spectacles like Mr Pickwick, who subscribes to all the war charities and is never tired of telling his friends what he would do with the Kaiser if he caught him."

I laughed aloud at this happy description of a typical John Bull.

"Well," he continued, "I suggested to Schumann the wild idea – as it seemed to us at first – of getting into the islands in the guise of a candidate for the parish of Myredale. Two days later Schumann came to me with his spectacles twinkling with excitement.

" 'Look at this!' said he.

"He showed me a photograph in an illustrated paper. It was the portrait of a certain Mr Alexander Burnett, minister of a parish in the south of Scotland, and I assure you that if the name 'Adolph Tiel' had been printed underneath, none of my friends would have questioned its being my own portrait.

" 'The stars are fighting for us!' said Schumann.

" 'They seem ready to enlist,' I agreed.

" 'How shall we encourage them?' said he.

" 'I shall let you know to-morrow,' I said.

"I went home and thought over the problem. From the first I was convinced that the only method which gave us a chance of success was for this man Burnett to enter voluntarily as a candidate, make all the arrangements himself – including the vital matter of a passport – and finally start actually upon his journey. Otherwise, no attempt to impersonate him seemed to me to stand any chance of success.

"Next day I saw Schumann and laid down these conditions, and we set about making preliminary inquiries. They were distinctly promising. Burnett's parish was a poor one, and from what we could gather, he had already been thinking for some time past of making a change.

"We began by sending him anonymously a paper containing a notice of the vacancy here. That of course was just to set him thinking about it. The next Sunday Schumann motored down to his parish, saw for himself that the resemblance to me was actually quite remarkable, and then after service made the minister's acquaintance. Imagine the good Mr Burnett's surprise and interest when this pleasant stranger proved to be intimately acquainted with the vacant parish of Myredale, and described it as a second Garden of Eden! Before they parted Schumann saw that the fish was hooked.

"The next problem was how to make the real Burnett vanish into space, and substitute the false Burnett without raising a trace of suspicion till my visit here was safely over. Again luck was with us. We sent an agent down to make inquiries of his servant a few days before he started, and found that he was going to spend a night with a friend in Edinburgh on his way north."

Tiel paused to knock the ashes out of his pipe, and I remarked –

"At first sight I confess that seems to me to complicate the problem. You would have to wait till Burnett had left Edinburgh, wouldn't you?"

Tiel smiled and shook his head.

"That is what we thought ourselves at first," said he, "but our second thoughts were better. What do you think of a wire to Burnett from his friend in Edinburgh telling him that a Mr Taylor would call for him in his motor-car: plus a wire to the friend in Edinburgh from Mr Burnett regretting that his visit must be postponed?"

"Excellent!" I laughed.

"Each wire, I may add, contained careful injunctions not to reply. And I may also add that the late Mr Burnett was simplicity itself."

I started involuntarily.

"The 'late' Mr Burnett! Do you mean–?"

"What else could one do with him?" asked Tiel calmly. "Both Schumann and I believe in being thorough."

Of course this worthy pair were but doing their duty. Still I was glad to think they had done their dirty work without my assistance. It was with a conscious effort that I was able to ask calmly–

"How did you manage it?"

"Mr Taylor, with his car and his chauffeur, called at the manse. The chauffeur remained in the car, keeping his face unostentatiously concealed. Mr Taylor enjoyed the minister's hospitality till the evening had sufficiently fallen. Then we took him to Edinburgh by the coast road."

Tiel paused and looked at me, as though to see how I was enjoying the gruesome tale. I am afraid I made it pretty clear that I was not enjoying it in the least. The idea of first partaking of the wretched man's hospitality, and then coolly murdering him, was a little too much for my stomach. Tiel, however, seemed rather amused than otherwise with my attitude.

"We knocked him on the head at a quiet part of the road, stripped him of every stitch of clothing, tied a large stone to his feet, and pitched him over the cliff," he said calmly.

"And his clothes–," I began, shrinking back a little in my chair.

"Are these," said Tiel, indicating his respectable-looking suit of black.

Curiously enough this was the only time I heard the man tell a tale of this sort, and in this diabolical, deliberate, almost flippant way. It was in marked contrast to his usually brief, concise manner of speaking. Possibly it was my reception of his story that discouraged him from exhibiting this side of his nature again. I certainly made no effort to conceal my distaste now.

"Thank God, I am not in the secret service!" I said devoutly.

"I understand you are in the submarine service," said Tiel in a dry voice.

" I am – and I am proud of it!"

"Have you never fired a torpedo at an inoffensive merchant ship?"

"That is very different!" I replied hotly.

"It is certainly more wholesale," said he.

I sprang up.

"Mr Tiel," I said, "kindly understand that a German naval officer is not in the habit of enduring affronts to his service!"

"But you think a German secret-service agent should have no such pride?" he inquired.

"I decline to discuss the question any further," I said stiffly.

For a moment he seemed exceedingly amused. Then he saw that I was in no humour for jesting on the subject, and he ceased to smile.

"Have another cigar?" he said, in a quiet matter-of-fact voice, just as though nothing had happened to ruffle the harmony of the evening.

"You quite understand what I said?" I demanded in an icy voice.

"I thought the subject was closed," he replied with a smile, and then jumping up he laid his hand on my arm in the friendliest fashion. "My dear Belke," said he, "we are going to be shut up together in this house for several days, and if we begin with a quarrel we shall certainly end in murder. Let us respect one another's point of view, and say no more about it."

" I don't know what you mean by 'one another's point of view,' " I answered politely but coldly. "So far as I am aware there is only *one* point of view, and I have just stated it. If we both respect that, there will be no danger of our quarrelling."

He glanced at me for a moment in an odd way, and then said merely –

"Well, are you going to have another cigar, or would you like to go to bed?"

"With your permission I shall go to bed," I said.

He conducted me through the hall and down the passage that led to the back premises. At the end rose a steep and narrow stair. We ascended this, and at the top found a narrow landing with a door at either end of it.

"This is your private flat," he explained in a low voice. "The old house, you will see, has been built in two separate instalments, which have separate stairs and no communication with one another on the upper landing. These two rooms are supposed to be locked up and not in use at present, but I have secured their keys."

He unlocked one of the doors, and we entered the room. It was square, and of quite a fair size. On two sides the walls sloped attic-wise, in a third was a fireplace and a window, and in the fourth two doors – the second opening into a large cupboard. This room had simple bedroom furniture, and also a small table and a basket chair. When we entered, it was lit only by a good fire, and pervaded by a pleasant aroma of peat smoke. Tiel lighted a paraffin lamp and remarked–

"You ought to be quite comfortable here."

Personally, I confess that my breath was fairly taken away. I had anticipated sleeping under the roof in some dark and chilly garret, or perhaps in the straw of an outhouse.

"Comfortable!" I exclaimed. "Mein Gott, who would not be on secret service! But are you sure all this is safe? This fire, for instance – the smoke surely will be seen."

"I have promised to keep the bedrooms aired while I am staying here," smiled Tiel.

He then explained in detail the arrangements of our remarkable household. He himself slept in the front part of the house, up the other staircase. The room opposite mine was empty, and so was the room underneath; but below the other was the kitchen, and I was warned to be very quiet in my movements. The single servant arrived early in the morning, and left about nine o'clock at night: she lived, it seemed, at a neighbouring farm; and Tiel assured me there was nothing to be feared from her provided I was reasonably careful.

I had brought with me a razor, a tooth-brush, and a brush and comb, and Tiel had very thoughtfully brought a spare sleeping suit and a pair of slippers. I was not at all sure that I was disposed to like the man, but I had to admit that his thoroughness and his consideration for my comfort were highly praiseworthy. In fact, I told him so frankly, and we parted for the night on friendly terms.

Tiel quietly descended the stairs, while I sat down before my fire and smoked a last cigarette, and then very gratefully turned into my comfortable bed.

III. – THE PLAN.

I SLEPT like a log, and only awakened when Tiel came into my room next morning, bringing my breakfast on a tray. He had sent the servant over to the farm for milk, he explained, and while I ate he sat down beside my bed.

"Can you talk business now?" I asked.

"This afternoon," said he.

I made a grimace.

"I naturally don't want to waste my time," I observed.

"You won't," he assured me.

"But why this afternoon rather than this morning? You can send the servant out for a message whenever you choose."

"I hope to have a pleasant little surprise for you in the afternoon."

I was aware of the fondness of these secret-service agents for a bit of mystery, and I knew I had to humour him. But really it seems a childish kind of vanity.

"There is one thing you can do for me," I said. "If I am to kick up my heels in this room all day – and probably for several days – I must have a pen and ink and some foolscap."

After his fashion he asked no questions but merely nodded, and presently brought them.

The truth was, I had conceived the idea of writing some account of my adventure, and in fact I am writing these lines now in that very bedroom I have described. I am telling a story of which I don't know the last chapter myself. A curious position for an author! If I am caught – well, it will make no difference. I have given nothing away that won't inevitably be discovered if I am arrested. And, mein Gott, what a relief it has been! I should have died of boredom otherwise.

If only my window looked out to sea! But, unluckily, I am at the back of the house and look, as it were sideways, on to a sloping hillside of green ferns below and brown heather at the top. By opening the window and putting my head right out, I suppose I should catch a glimpse of the sea, but then my neighbours would catch a glimpse of me. I expostulated with Tiel as soon as I realised how the room faced, but he points out that the servant may go into any room in the front part of the house, whereas this part is supposed to be closed. I can see that he is right, but it is nevertheless very tantalising.

On that Saturday afternoon Tiel came back to my room some hours later, and under his quiet manner I could see that he bore tidings of importance. No one could come quicker to the point when he chose, and this time he came to it at once.

"You remember the affair of the *Haileybury*?" he demanded.

"The British cruiser which was mined early in the war?"

He nodded.

"Perfectly," I said.

"You never at any time came across her captain? His name was Ashington."

"No," I said, "I have met very few British officers."

"I don't know whether you heard that she was supposed to be two miles out of her proper course, contrary to orders, did you?"

"Was she?"

"Ashington says 'no.' But he was court-martialled, and now he's in command of a small boat – the *Yellowhammer*. Before the loss of his ship he was considered one of the most promising officers in the British service; now–!"

Tiel made an expressive gesture and his eyes smiled at me oddly. I began to understand.

"Now he is an acquaintance of yours?"

Tiel nodded.

"But has he knowledge? Has he special information?"

"His younger brother is on the flagship, and he has several very influential friends. I see that *my* friends obtain knowledge."

I looked at him hard.

"You are *quite* sure this is all right? Such men are the last to be trusted – even by those who pay them."

"Do you know many 'such men'?" he inquired.

"None, I am thankful to say."

"They are queer fish," said Tiel in a reminiscent way, " but they generally do the thing pretty thoroughly, especially when one has a firm enough hold of them. Ashington is absolutely reliable."

"Where is he to be seen?"

"He went out for a walk this afternoon," said Tiel drily, "and happened to call at the manse to see if he could get a cup of tea – a very natural thing to do. Come – the coast is clear."

He led the way downstairs and I followed him, not a little excited, I confess. How my mission was going to develop, I had no dear idea when I set forth upon it, but though I had imagined several possible developments, I was not quite prepared for this. To have an officer of the Grand Fleet actually assisting at our councils was decidedly unexpected. I began to realise more and more that Adolph Tiel was a remarkable person.

In the front parlour an officer rose as we entered, and the British and German uniforms bowed to each other under circumstances which were possibly unique. Because, though Ashingtons do exist and these things sometimes happen, they generally happen in mufti. I looked at our visitor very hard. On his part, he looked at me sharply for a moment, and then averted his eyes. I should certainly have done the same in his place.

He was a big burly man, dark, and getting bald. His voice was deep and rich; his skin shone with physical fitness; altogether he was a fine gross animal, and had his spirit been as frank and jovial as his appearance suggested, I could have pictured him the jolliest of company in the ward-room and the life and soul of a desperate enterprise. But he maintained a frowning aspect, and was clearly a man whose sullen temper and sense of injury had led him into my friend's subtle net. However, here he was, and it was manifestly my business not to criticise but to make the most of him.

"Well, gentlemen," began Tiel, "I don't think we need beat about the bush. Captain Ashington has an idea, and it is for Lieutenant von Belke to approve of it or not. I know enough myself about naval affairs to see that there are great possibilities in the suggestion, but I don't know enough to advise on it."

"What is the suggestion?" I asked in a very dry and non-committal voice.

Captain Ashington, I noticed, cleared his throat before he began.

"The fleet is going out one evening next week," he said; "probably on Thursday."

"How do you know?" I demanded.

He looked confidentially at Tiel.

"Mr Tiel knows the source of my information," he said.

"I should like to know it too," said I.

"I can vouch for Captain Ashington's information," said Tiel briefly.

There is something extraordinarily decisive and satisfying about Tiel when he speaks like that. I knew it must be all right; still, I felt it my duty to make sure.

"Have you any objections to telling me?" I asked. Tiel stepped to my side and whispered –

"I told you about his brother."

I understood, and did not press my question. Whether to respect the man for this remnant of delicacy, or to despise him for not being a more thorough, honest blackguard, I was not quite sure.

"Well," I said, "suppose we know when they are going out, they will take the usual precautions, I presume?" Ashington leaned forward confidentially over the table.

"They are going out on a new course," he said in a low voice.

I pricked up my ears, but all I said was

"Why is that?"

"On account of the currents. The old passage hasn't been quite satisfactory. They are going to experiment with a new passage."

This certainly sounded all right, for I knew how diabolical the tideways can be round these islands.

"Do you know the new course at all accurately?" I inquired.

Captain Ashington smiled for the first time, and somehow or other the sight of a smile on his face gave me a strongly increased distaste for the man.

"I know it exactly," he said.

He took out of his pocket a folded chart and laid it on the table. The three of us bent over it, and at a glance I could see that this was business indeed. All the alterations in the mine-fields were shown and the course precisely laid down.

"Well," said Tiel, "I think this suggests something, Belke."

By this time I was inwardly burning with excitement.

"I hope to have the pleasure of being present just about that spot," I said, pointing to the chart.

"Or there," suggested Ashington.

"Either would do very nicely, so far as I can judge," said Tiel. "How many submarines can you concentrate, and how long will it take you to concentrate them?"

I considered the question.

"I am afraid there is no use in concentrating more than two or three in such narrow waters," I said. "Squadronal handling of submarines of course is impossible except on the surface. And we clearly can't keep on the surface!"

Captain Ashington looked at me in a way I did not at all like.

"We run a few risks in the British navy," he said. " D—n it, you'll have a sitting target! I'd crowd in every blank submarine the water would float if I were running this stunt!"

"You don't happen to be running it," I said coldly.

Tiel touched me lightly on the shoulder and gave me a swift smile, pleasant but admonitory.

"The happy mean seems to be suggested," he said soothingly. "There's a great deal to be said for both points of view. On the one hand you risk submarines: on the other hand you make the battle-fleet run risks. One has simply to balance those. What about half a dozen submarines?"

I shook my head.

"Too many," I said. "Besides, we couldn't concentrate them in the time."

"How many could you?"

"Four," I said; "if I can get back to my boat on Monday, we'll have them there on Thursday."

Tiel produced a bottle of whisky and syphons and we sat over the chart discussing details for some time longer. It was finally handed over to me, and Captain Ashington rose to go.

"By the way," I said, "there is one very important preliminary to be arranged. How am I to get back to my boat?"

"That will be all right," said Tiel confidently; "I have just heard from Captain Ashington that they have arrested the wrong man on suspicion of being the gentleman who toured the country yesterday. The only thing is that they can't find his cycle. Now I think if we could arrange to have your motor-cycle quietly left near his house and discovered by the authorities, they are not likely to watch the roads any longer."

"I'll fix that up," said Captain Ashington promptly.

"How will you manage it?" I asked.

"Trust him," said Tiel.

"But then how shall I get back?"

"I shall drive you over," smiled Tiel. "There will probably be a dying woman who desires the consolations of religion in that neighbourhood on Monday night."

I smiled too, but merely at the cunning of the man, not at the thought of parting with my motor-cycle. However, I saw perfectly well that it would be folly to ride it over, and if I left it behind at the manse – well, I was scarcely likely to call for it again!

"Now, Belke," said Tiel, "we had better get you safely back to your turret chamber. You have been away quite as long as is safe."

I bowed to Captain Ashington – I could not bring myself to touch his hand, and we left his great gross figure sipping whisky-and-soda.

"What do you think of him?" asked Tiel.

"He seems extremely competent," I answered candidly. "But what an unspeakable scoundrel!"

"We mustn't quarrel with our instruments," said he philosophically. "He is doing Germany a good turn. Surely that is enough."

"I should like to think that Germany did not need to stoop to use such characters!"

"Yes," he agreed, though in a colourless voice, "one would indeed like to think so."

I could see that Adolph Tiel had not many scruples left after his cosmopolitan experiences.

IV. – WHAT HAPPENED ON SUNDAY.

THAT EVENING when we had the house to ourselves, I joined Tiel in the parlour, and we had a long talk on naval matters, British and German. He knew less of British naval affairs than I did, but quite enough about German to make him a keen listener and a very suggestive talker. In fact I found him excellent company. I even suspected him at last of being a man of good birth, and quite fitting company for a German officer. But of course he may have acquired his air of breeding from mixing with men like myself. As for his name, that of course gave no guide, for I scarcely supposed that he had been Tiel throughout his adventurous career. I threw out one or two 'feelers' on the subject, but no oyster could be more secretive than Adolph Tiel when he chose.

That night I heard the wind wandering noisily round the old house, and I wakened in the morning to find the rain beating on the window. Tiel came in rather late with my breakfast, and I said to him at once –

"I have just remembered that this is Sunday. I wish I could come and hear your sermon, Tiel!"

"I wish you could, too," said he. "It will be a memorable event in the parish."

"But are you actually going to do it?"

"How can I avoid it?"

"You are so ingenious I should have thought you would have hit upon a plan."

He looked at me in his curious way.

"Why should I have tried to get out of it?" I shrugged my shoulders.

"Personally, I shouldn't feel anxious to make a mock of religion if I could avoid it."

"We are such a religious people," said he, "that surely we can count on God forgiving us more readily than other nations."

He spoke in his driest voice, and for a moment I looked at him suspiciously. But he was perfectly grave.

"Still," I replied, "I am glad the Navy doesn't have to preach bogus sermons!"

"Ah," said he, "the German navy has to keep on its pedestal. But the secret service must sometimes creep about in the dust."

His eyes suddenly twinkled as he added –

"But never fear, I shall give them a beautiful sermon! The text will be the passage about Joshua and the spies, and the first hymn will be, 'Onward, Christian Sailors.' "

He threw me a humorous glance and went out. I smiled back, but I confess I was not very much amused. Neither the irreverence nor the jest about the sailors (since it referred apparently to me) struck me as in the best of taste.

That morning was one of the dreariest I ever spent. The wind rose to half a gale, and the fine rain beat in torrents on the panes. I wrote diligently for some time, but after a while I grew tired of that and paced the floor in my stockinged feet (for the sake of quietness) like a caged animal. My one consolation was that to-morrow would see the end of my visit. Already I longed for the cramped quarters and perpetual risks of the submarine, and detested these islands even more bitterly than I hated any other part of Britain.

In the early afternoon I had a pleasant surprise. Tiel came in and told me that his servant had gone out for the rest of the day, and that I could safely come down to the parlour. There I had a late luncheon in comparative comfort, and moreover I could look out of the windows on to the sea. And what a dreary prospect I saw! Under a heavy sky and with grey showers rolling over it, that open treeless country looked desolation itself. As for the waters, whitecaps chased each other over the wind-whipped expanse of grey, fading into a wet blur of moving rain a few miles out. Through this loomed the nearer lines of giant ships, while the farther were blotted clean out. I thought of the long winters when one day of this weather followed another for week after week, month after month; when the northern days were brief and the nights interminable, and this armada lay in these remote isles enduring and waiting. The German navy has had its gloomy and impatient seasons, but not such a prolonged purgatory as that. We have a different arrangement. Probably everybody knows what it is – still, one must not say.

After lunch, when we had lit our cigars, Tiel said –

"By the way, you will be pleased to hear that my efforts this morning were so successful that the people want me to give them another dose next Sunday."

I stared at him.

"Really?" I exclaimed. He nodded.

"But I thought there would be another preacher next Sunday."

"Oh, by no means. There was no one for next Sunday, and they were only too glad to have the pulpit filled."

"But will you risk it?"

He smiled confidently.

"If there is any danger, I shall get warning in plenty of time."

"To ensure your escape?"

"To vanish somehow,"

"But why should you wait?"

He looked at me seriously and said deliberately —

"I have other schemes in my head – something even bigger. It is too early to talk yet, but it is worth running a little risk for."

I looked at this astonishing man with unconcealed admiration. Regulations, authorities, precautions, dangers, he seemed to treat as almost negligible, And I had seen how he could contrive and what he could effect.

"I am afraid I shall have to ask you to stay with me for a few days longer," he added.

I don't think I ever got a more unpleasant shock.

"You mean you wish me *not* to rejoin my ship to-morrow night?"

" I know it is asking a great deal of you; but, my dear Belke, duty is duty."

"My duty is with my ship," I said quickly. "Besides, it is the post of danger – and of honour. Think of Thursday night!"

"Do you honestly think you are essential to the success of a torpedo attack?"

"Every officer will be required."

"My dear Belke, you didn't answer my question. Are you *essential*?"

"My dear Tiel," I replied firmly, for I was quite resolved I should not remain cooped up in this infernal house, exposed to hourly risk of being shot as a spy, while my ship was going into action, "I am sorry to seem disobliging; but I am a naval officer, and my first duty is quite clear to me."

"Pardon me for reminding you that you are at present under my orders," said he.

"While this affair is being arranged only."

"But I say that I have not yet finished my arrangements." I saw that I was in something of a dilemma, for indeed it was difficult to say exactly how my injunctions met the case.

"Well," I said, "I shall tell you what I shall do. I shall put it to my superior officer, Commander Wiedermann, and ask him whether he desires me to absent myself any longer."

This was a happy inspiration, for I felt certain what Wiedermann would say.

"Then I shall not know till to-morrow night whether to count on you – and then I shall very probably lose you?"

I shrugged my shoulders, but said nothing. Suddenly his face cleared.

"My dear fellow," he said, "I won't press you. Rejoin your ship if you think it your duty."

By mutual consent we changed the subject, and discussed the question of submarines *versus* surface ships, a subject in which Tiel showed both interest and acumen, though I had naturally more knowledge, and could contribute much from my own personal experience. I must add that it is a pleasure to discuss such matters with him, for he has a frank and genuine respect for those who really understand what they are talking about.

Towards evening I went back to my room, and fell to writing this narrative again, but about ten o'clock I had another visit from Tiel; and again he disconcerted me, though not so seriously this time.

"I had a message from Ashington, asking to see me," he explained, "and I have just returned from a meeting with him. He tells me that the date of the fleet's sailing will probably be altered to Friday, but he will let me know definitely to-morrow or Tuesday."

"Or Tuesday!" I exclaimed. "Then I may have to stay here for another night!"

"I'm sorry," said he, "but I'm afraid it can't be helped."

"But can we ever be sure that the fleet will keep to a programme? I have just been thinking it over, and the question struck me – why are they making this arrangement so far ahead?"

"That struck me too," said Tiel, "and also Ashington. But he has found out now. There is some big scheme on. Some think it is Heligoland, and some think the Baltic. Anyhow, there is a definite programme, and they will certainly keep to it. The only uncertain thing is the actual day of sailing."

"It is a plan which will be nicely upset if we get our torpedoes into three or four of their super-dreadnoughts!" I exclaimed.

He nodded grimly.

"And for that, we want to have the timing *exact*," he said. "Be patient, my friend; we shall know by Tuesday morning at the latest."

I tried to be as philosophical as I could, but it was a dreary evening, with the rain still beating on my window and another day's confinement to look forward to.

V. – A MYSTERIOUS ADVENTURE.

MONDAY morning broke wet and windy, but with every sign of clearing up. Tiel looked in for a very few minutes, but he was in his most uncommunicative mood, and merely told me that he would have to be out for the first part of the day, but would be back in the afternoon. I could not help suspecting that he was still a little sore over my refusal to remain with him, and was paying me out by this display of secrecy. Such petty affronts to officers from those unfortunate enough to be outside that class are not unknown. I was of course above taking offence, but I admit that it made me feel less anxious to consult his wishes at every turn.

In this humour I wrote for a time, and at last got up and stared impatiently out of the window. It had become quite a fine day, and the prospect of gazing for the greater part of it at a few acres of inland landscape, with that fascinating spectacle to be seen from the front windows, irritated me more and more. And then, to add to my annoyance, I heard "Boom! Boom! Boom!" crashing from the seaward side, and shaking the very foundations of the house. I began to feel emphatically that it was my duty to watch the British fleet at gunnery practice.

Just then two women appeared, walking slowly away from the house. One had an apron and no hat, and though I had only once caught a fleeting glimpse of the back view of our servant, I made quite certain it was she. I watched them till they reached a farm about quarter of a mile away, and turned into the house, and then I said to myself –

"There can be no danger now!"

And thereupon I unlocked my door, walked boldly downstairs, and went into the front parlour.

I saw a vastly different scene from yesterday. A fresh breeze rippled the blue waters, patches of sunshine and cloud-shadow chased each other over sea and land, and distinct and imposing in its hateful majesty lay the British fleet. A light cruiser of an interesting new type was firing her 6-inch guns at a distant target, and for about five minutes I thoroughly enjoyed myself. And then I heard a sound.

I turned instantly, to see the door opening; and very hurriedly I stepped back behind the nearest window curtain. And then in came our servant – *not* the lady I had seen departing from the house, I need scarcely say! I was fully half exposed and I dared not make a movement to draw the curtain round me; in fact, even if I had, my feet would have remained perfectly visible. All I could do was to stand as still as a statue and pray that Heaven would blind her.

She walked in briskly, a middle-aged capable-looking woman, holding a broom, and glanced all round the room in a purposeful way. Among the things she looked at was me, but to my utter astonishment she paid no more attention than if I had been a piece of furniture. For a moment I thought she was blind; but her sharp glances clearly came from no sightless eyes. Then I wondered whether she could have such a horrible squint that when she seemed to look at me she was really looking in another direction. But I could see no sign of a cast in those eyes either. And then she picked up an armful of small articles and walked quickly out, leaving the door wide open.

What had saved me I had no idea, but I was resolved not to trust to that curtain any longer. In the middle of the room was a square table of moderate size with a cloth over it. Without stopping to think twice, I dived under the cloth and crouched upon the floor.

The next instant in she came again, and I found that my table-cloth was so scanty that I could follow her movements perfectly. She took some more things out, and then more again, and finally she proceeded to set the furniture piece by piece back against the wall, till the table was left lonely and horribly conspicuous in the middle of the floor. And then she began to sweep out that room.

There was small scope for an exhibition of resource, but I was as resourceful as I was able. I very gently pulled the scanty table-cloth first in one direction and then in the other, according to the side of the room she was sweeping, and as noiselessly as possible I crept a foot or two farther away from her each time. And all the while the dust rose in clouds, and the hateful broom came so near me that it sometimes brushed my boots. And yet the extraordinary woman never showed by a single sign that she had any suspicion of my presence!

At last when the whole floor had been swept – except of course under the table – she paused, and from the glimpse I could get of her attitude she seemed to be ruminating. And then she stooped, lifted the edge of the cloth, and said in an absolutely matter-of-fact voice–

"Will you not better get out till I'm through with my sweeping?"

Too utterly bewildered to speak, I crept out and rose to my feet.

"You can get under the table again when I'm finished," she observed as she pulled off the cloth.

To such an observation there seemed no adequate reply, or at least I could think of none. I turned in silence and hurried back to my bedroom. And there I sat for a space too dumfounded for coherent thought.

Gradually I began to recover my wits and ponder over this mysterious affair, and a theory commenced to take shape. Clearly she was insane, or at least half-witted, and was quite incapable of drawing reasonable conclusions. And the more I thought it over, the more did several circumstances seem to confirm this view. My fire, for instance, with its smoke coming out of the chimney, and the supply of peat and firewood which Tiel or I were constantly bringing up. Had she noticed nothing of that? Also Tiel's frequent ascents of this back staircase to a part of the house supposed to be closed. She must be half-witted.

And then I began to recall her brisk eye and capable air, and the idiot theory resolved into space. Only one alternative seemed left. She must be spying upon us, and aware of my presence all the time! But if so, what could I do? I felt even more helpless than I did that first night when my motor-cycle broke down. I could only sit and wait, revolver in hand.

When I heard Tiel's step at last on the stairs, I confess that my nerves were not at their best.

"We are betrayed!" I exclaimed.

He stared at me very hard.

"What do you mean?" he asked quietly, and I am bound to say this of Tiel, that there is something very reassuring in his calm voice.

I told him hurriedly. He looked at me for a moment, began to smile, and then checked himself.

"I owe you an apology, Belke," he said. "I ought to have explained that that woman is in my pay."

"In your pay?" I cried. "And she has been so all the time?"

He nodded.

"And yet you never told me, but let me hide up in this room like a rat in a hole?"

"The truth is," he replied, "that till I had got to know you pretty well, I was afraid you might be rash – or at least careless, if you knew that woman was one of us."

"So you treated me like an infant, Mr Tiel?"

"The life I have lived," said Tiel quietly, "has not been conducive to creating a feeling of confidence in my fellowmen's discretion – until I *know* them. I know you now, and I feel sorry I took this precaution. Please accept my apologies."

"I accept your apology," I said stiffly; "but in future, Mr Tiel, things will be pleasanter if you trust me."

He bowed slightly and said simply —

"I shall."

And then in a different voice he said—

"We have a visitor coming this afternoon to stay with us."

"To stay here!" I exclaimed.

"Another of *us*," he explained.

"Another – in these islands? Who is he?"

As I spoke we heard a bell ring.

"Ah, here she is," said Tiel, going to the door. "Come down and be introduced whenever you like."

For a moment I stood stock still, lost in doubt and wonder.

"She!" I repeated to myself.

VI.-THE VISITOR.

MY feelings as I approached the parlour were anything but happy. Some voice seemed to warn me that I was in the presence of something sinister, that some unknown peril stalked at my elbow. This third party – this "she" – filled me with forebodings. If ever anybody had a presentiment, I had one, and all I can say now is that within thirty seconds of opening the parlour door, I had ceased to believe in presentiments, entirely and finally. The vision I beheld nearly took my breath away.

"Let me introduce you to my sister, Miss Burnett," said Tiel. "She is so devoted to her brother that she has insisted on coming to look after him for the few days he is forced to spend in this lonely manse."

He said this with a smile, and of course never intended me to believe a word of his statement, yet as he gave her no other name, and as that was the only account of her circulated in the neighbourhood, I shall simply refer to her in the meantime as Miss Burnett. It is the only name that I have to call her by to her face.

As to her appearance, I can only say that she is the most beautiful woman I have ever met in my life. The delicacy and distinction of her features, her dark eyebrows, her entrancing eye, and her thoughtful mouth, so firm and yet so sweet, her delicious figure and graceful carriage – heavens, I have never seen any girl to approach her! What is more, she has a face which I *trust*. I have had some experience of women, and I could feel at the first exchange of glances and of words that here was one of those rare women on whom a man could implicitly rely.

"Have you just landed upon these islands?" I inquired.

"Not to-day," she said; and indeed, when I came to think of it, she would not have had time to reach the house in that case.

"Did you have much difficulty?" I asked.

"The minister's sister is always admitted," said Tiel with his dry smile.

I asked presently if she had travelled far. She shrugged her shoulders, gave a delightful little laugh, and said–

"We get so used to travelling that I have forgotten what 'far' is!"

Meanwhile tea was brought in, and Miss Burnett sat down and poured it out with the graceful nonchalant air of a charming hostess in her own drawing-room, while Tiel talked of the weather and referred carelessly to the latest news just like any gentleman who might have called casually upon her. I, on my part, tried as best I could to catch the same air, and we all talked away very pleasantly indeed. We spoke English, of course, all the time, and indeed, any one overhearing us and not seeing my uniform would never have dreamt for a moment that we were anything but three devoted subjects of King George.

On the other hand, we were surely proceeding on the assumption that nobody was behind a curtain or listening at the keyhole, and that being so, I could not help feeling that the elaborate pretence of being a mere party of ordinary acquaintances was a little unnecessary. At last I could not help saying something of what was in my mind.

"Is the war over?" I asked suddenly. Both the others seemed surprised.

"I wish it were, Mr Belke!" said Miss Burnett with a sudden and moving change to seriousness.

"Then if it is not, why are we pretending so religiously that we have no business here but to drink tea, Miss Burnett?"

"I am not pretending; I am drinking it," she smiled.

"Yes, yes," I said, "but you know what I mean. It seems to me so un-German!"

They both looked at me rather hard.

"I'm afraid," said Miss Burnett, "that we of the secret service grow terribly cosmopolitan. Our habits are those of no country – or rather of all countries."

"I had almost forgotten," said Tiel, "that I once thought and felt like Mr Belke." And then he added this singular opinion: "It is Germany's greatest calamity – greater even than the coming in of Britain against her, or the Battle of the Marne – that those who guide her destinies have not forgotten it too."

"What do you mean?" I demanded, a little indignantly I must own.

"At every tea-party for many years Germany has talked about what interested herself – and that was chiefly war. At no tea-party has she tried to learn the thoughts and interests of the other guests. In consequence she does not yet understand the forces against her, why they act as they do, and how strong they are. But her enemies understand too well."

"You mean that she has been honest and they dishonest?"

"Yes," said Miss Burnett promptly and with a little smile, "my brother means that in order really to deceive people one has to act as we are acting now."

I laughed.

"But unfortunately now there is no one to deceive!" She laughed too.

"But they might suddenly walk in!"

Tiel was not a frequent laugher, but he condescended to smile.

"Remember, Belke," he said, "I warned you on the first night we met that you must not only talk but think in English. If we don't do that constantly and continually when no one is watching us, how can we count on doing it constantly and continually when someone *may* be watching us?"

"Personally I should think it sufficient to wait till some one *was* watching," I said.

"There speaks Germany," smiled Tiel.

"Germany disdains to act a part all the time!" I cried.

I confess I was nettled by his tone, but his charming 'sister' disarmed me instantly.

"Mr Belke means that he wants footlights and an orchestra and an audience before he mutters 'Hush! I hear her coming!' He doesn't believe in saying 'Hush!' in the corner of every railway carriage or under his umbrella. And I really think it makes him much less alarming company!"

"You explain things very happily, Eileen," said Tiel.

I was watching her face (for which there was every excuse!) and I saw that she started ever so slightly when he called her by her first name. This pleased me – I must confess it. It showed that they had not played this farce of brother and sister together before, and already I had begun to dislike a little the idea that they were old and intimate confederates. I also fancied that it showed she did not quite enjoy the familiarity. But she got her own back again instantly.

"It is my one desire to enlighten you, Alexander," she replied with a very serious air.

I could not help laughing aloud, and I must confess that Tiel laughed frankly too.

The next question that I remember our discussing was one of very immediate and vital interest to us all. It began with a remark by Eileen (as I simply must call her behind her back; 'Miss Burnett' smacks too much of Tiel's disguises – and besides it is too British). We were talking of the English, and she said–

"Well, anyhow they are not a very suspicious people. Look at this little party!"

"Sometimes I feel that they are almost incredibly unsuspicious," I said seriously. "In Germany this house would surely be either visited or watched!"

Tiel shook his head.

"In Keil or Wilhelmshaven an English party could live just as unmolested," he replied, "provided that not the least trace of suspicion was aroused *at the outset*. That is the whole secret of my profession. One takes advantages of the fact that even the most wary and watchful men take the greater part of their surroundings for granted. The head of any War Office – German, French, English, or whatever it may be – doesn't suddenly conceive a suspicion of one of his clerks, unless something in the clerk's conduct calls his attention. If, then, it were possible to enter the War Office, looking and behaving exactly like one of the clerks, suspicion would not *begin*. It is the beginning one has to guard against."

"Why don't you enter the British War Office, then?" asked Eileen with a smile.

"Because, unfortunately, they know all the clerks intimately by sight. In this case they expected a minister whom nobody knew. The difficulty of the passport with its photograph was got over by a little ingenuity." (He threw me a quick grim smile.) "Thus I was able to appear as a person fully expected, and as long as I don't do anything inconsistent with the character, why should anyone throw even so much as an inquisitive glance in my direction. Until suspicion *begins*, we are as safe here as in the middle of Berlin. Once it begins – well, it will be a very different story."

"And you don't think my coming will rouse any suspicion?" asked Eileen, with, for the first time (I fancied), a faint suggestion of anxiety.

"Suspicion? Certainly not! Just think. Put yourself in the shoes of the neighbours in the parish, or even of any naval officer who might chance to learn you were here. What is more natural than that the minister who – at the request of the people – is staying a week longer than he intended, should get his sister to look after him? The danger-point in both cases was passed when we got into the islands. We know that there was no suspicion roused in either case."

"How do you know?" I interposed.

"Another quality required for this work," replied Tiel with a detached air, "is enough imagination to foresee the precautions that will be required. One wants to establish precaution behind precaution, just as an army establishes a series of defensive positions. In this case I have got our good friend Ashington watching closely for the first evidence of doubt or inquiry. So that I *know* that both my sister and I passed the barrier without raising a question in anybody's mind."

"But how do you know that Ashington can be absolutely relied on?" I persisted.

"Yes," put in Eileen, "I was wondering too."

"Because Ashington will certainly share my fate – whatever that may be," said Tiel grimly. "He knows that; in fact he knows that I have probably taken steps to ensure that happening, in case there might be any loophole for him."

"But can't a man turn King's evidence (isn't that the term?) and get pardoned?" asked Eileen.

"Not a naval officer," said Tiel.

"No," I agreed. "I must say that for the British Navy. An officer would have no more chance of pardon in it than in our own navy."

"Well," smiled Eileen, "I feel relieved! Don't you, Mr Belke?"

"Yes," I said, "I begin to understand the whole situation more clearly. I pray that suspicion may not *begin*!"

"In that case," said Tiel, "you realise now, perhaps, why we have to keep up acting, whether any one is watching us or not"

"Yes," I admitted, "I begin to see your reasons a little better. But why didn't you tell me all this before?"

"All what?".

"Well – about Ashington, for instance."

"I suppose," he said, "the truth is, Belke, that you have laid your finger on another instance of people taking things for granted. I assumed you would realise these things. It was my own fault."

It was on the tip of my tongue to tell him that the real reason was his love of mystery and his Secret Service habit of distrusting people, but I realised that Eileen had shown a little of the same evasiveness, and I would not have her think that my criticism was directed against her.

Presently Tiel suggested that it would be wiser if I retired to my room, and for a moment there was a sharp, though politely expressed difference of opinion between us. I argued very naturally that since the servant was in our pay there was no danger to be apprehended within the house, and that I was as safe in the parlour as anywhere. In his *mystery-making*, ultra-cautious way, he insisted that a visitor *might* appear (he even suggested the police – though he had just previously said they had no suspicion!) and that he was going to run no risks. Eileen said a word on his side – though with a very kind look at me – and I consented to go. And then he requested me to stay there for the rest of the evening! Again Eileen saved a strained situation, and I said farewell stiffly to him and very differently to her; in fact I made a point of accentuating the difference.

I reached my room, lit a cigar, and for a time paced the floor in a state of mind which I found hard to analyse. I can only say that my feelings were both mixed and strong, and that at last, to give me relief, I sat down to write my narrative, and by nine o'clock in the evening had brought it up nearly to this point.

By that time of course the curtains were drawn and my lamp was lit, and as it was a windy chilly night, my fire was blazing brightly. Higher and higher rose the wind till it began to make a very heavy and constant booming in the chimney, like distant salvoes of great guns. Apart from the wind the old house was utterly quiet, and when the wooden stair suddenly creaked I dropped my pen and sat up very sharply. More and more distinctly I heard a firm but light tread coming up and up, until at last it ceased on the landing. And then came a gentle tap upon my door.

VII. – AT NIGHT.

WITH a curious sense of excitement I crossed the room. I opened the door – and there stood Eileen. She had taken off her hat, and without it looked even more beautiful, for what hat could rival her masses of dark hair so artfully arranged and yet with a rippling wave all through them that utterly defied restraint?

"May I come in for a little?" she said.

She asked in such a friendly smiling way, so modest and yet so unafraid, that even the greatest Don Juan could not have mistaken her honest intention.

"I shall be more than charmed to have your company," I said.

"I'm afraid we soon forget the conventionalities in our service," she said simply. "Tiel has gone out, and I was getting very tired of my own company."

"Imagine how tired I have got of mine!" I cried. She gave a little understanding nod.

"It must be dreadfully dull for you," she agreed with great sincerity – and she added, as she seated herself in my wicker chair, "I have another excuse for calling on you, and that is, that the more clearly we all three understand what we are doing, the better. Don't you think so?"

"Decidedly! In fact I only wish we all thought the same," She looked at me inquiringly, and yet as though she comprehended quite well.

"You mean–?"

"Well, to be quite frank, I mean Tiel. He is very clever, and he knows his work. Mein Gott, we can teach him nothing! And perhaps he trusts you implicitly and is quite candid. But he certainly tells me no more than he can help."

"He tells nobody more than he can help," she said. "You are no worse treated than anyone else he works with. But it is a little annoying sometimes."

"For instance, do you know what he is doing to-night?" I asked.

There was no mistaking the criticism in the little shrug with which she replied–

"I half suspect he is walking about in the dark by himself just to make me think he is busy on some mysterious affair!"

"Do you actually mean that?" I exclaimed.

"No, no," she said hastily, "not really quite that! I But he sometimes tempts one to say these things."

"Have you worked with him often before?"

"Enough to know his little peculiarities." She smiled suddenly. "Oh, he is a very wonderful man, is my dear brother!"

Again I was delighted (I confess it shamelessly!) to hear that unmistakable note of criticism.

" 'Wonderful' may have several meanings," I suggested. "It has in his case," she said frankly. "He really is extraordinarily clever."

She added nothing more, but the implication was very clear that the other meanings were not quite so flattering. I felt already that this strange little household was divided into two camps, and that Eileen and I were together in one.

"But we have talked enough about Herr Tiel!" she exclaimed in a different voice. "Because we really can get no further. It is like discussing what is inside a locked box! We can trust his judgment in this business; I think you will agree to that."

"Oh yes," I said, "I have seen enough to respect his abilities very thoroughly."

"Then," said she, "let us talk of something more amusing."

"Yourself," I said frankly, though perhaps a little too boldly, for she did not respond immediately. I felt that I had better proceed more diplomatically.

"I was wondering whether you were a pure German," I added.

"My feelings towards Germany are as strong as yours, Mr Belke," she answered. "Indeed I don't think any one can be more loyal to their country than I am, but I am not purely German by blood. My mother was Irish, hence my name – Eileen."

"Then that is your real name?" I cried, between surprise and delight.

"Yes, that is the one genuine thing about me," she smiled.

" But if you are half English–"

"Irish," she corrected.

"Ah!" I cried. "I see – of course! I was going to ask whether you sympathies were not at all divided. But Irish is very different. Then you hate the English with a double hatred?"

"With one or two exceptions – friends I have made – I abhor the whole race I am fighting against quite as much as you could possibly wish me to! Indeed, I wish it were fighting and not merely plotting!"

There was an earnestness and intensity in her voice and a kindling of her eye as she said this that thrilled and inspired me like a trumpet.

"We shall defeat them – never fear!" I cried. "We shall trample on the pride of England. It will be hard to do, but I have no doubt as to the result; have you?"

"None," she said, quietly but with absolute confidence. Then that quick smile of hers, a little grave but very charming, broke over her face.

"But let us get away for a little from war," she said. "You aren't smoking. Please do, if you wish to."

I lit a cigarette, and offered one to her, but she said she did not smoke. And I liked her all the better. We talked more lightly for a while, or perhaps I should rather say less earnestly, for our situation did not lend itself to frivolity. It did lend itself however to romance, – we two sitting on either side of the peat fire, with a shaded lamp and the friendly flames throwing odd lights and shadows through the low, primitive room with its sloping attic-like walls and its scanty furniture; and the wind all the while tempestuously booming in the chimney and scouring land and sea. And neither on land nor sea was there a single friend; surrounded by enemies who would have given a heavy price to have learned who sat in that room, we talked of many things.

At last, all too soon, she rose and wished me good-night.

A demon of perversity seized me.

"I shall escort you down to Mr Tiel, and the devil take his precautions!" I exclaimed.

"Oh no," she protested. "After all he is in command." She really seemed quite concerned at my intention, but I can be very obstinate when I choose.

"Tuts!" I said. "It is sheer rubbish to pretend that there is any risk at this time of night. Probably he is still out, and anyhow he will not have visitors at this hour."

She looked at me very hard and quickly as if to see if I were possible to argue with, and then she gave a little laugh and merely said–

"You are terribly wilful. Mr Belke!"

And she ran downstairs very quickly, as though to run away from me. I followed fast, but she was some paces ahead of me as we went down the dark passage to the front of the house. And then suddenly I heard guarded voices, and stopped dead.

There was a bend in the passage just before it reached the hall, and Eileen had passed this while I had not, and so I could see nothing ahead. Then I heard the voice of Tiel say–

"Well?"

It was a simple word of little significance, but the voice in which it was said filled me with a very unpleasant sensation. The man spoke in such a familiar confidential way that I suddenly felt I could have shot him cheerfully. For the instant I forgot the problem of the other voice I had heard.

"Mr Belke is with me! He insisted," she cried.

At this I knew that the unknown voice could not belong to an enemy, and I advanced again. As I passed the bend in the passage I was just in time to see Tiel closing the front door behind a man in a long dark coat with a gleam of brass buttons, and to hear him say,

"Good-night, Ashington."

Eileen passed into the parlour with a smiling glance for me to follow, and Tiel came in after us. I was not in the most pleasant temper. In fact, for some reason I was in a very black humour.

"I thought you had gone out," I said to him at once.

"I did go out."

"But now I understand that the worthy Captain Ashington has been visiting you here!"

"Both these remarkable events have occurred," said Tiel drily.

When I recalled how long Eileen had been up in my room, I realised that this was quite possible, but this did not, for some reason, soothe me.

"Why did he come?" I asked.

"The fleet is going out on Friday."

"Aha!" I exclaimed, forgetting my annoyance for the moment.

"So that is settled at last," said Tiel with a satisfied smile. He happened to turn his smile on Eileen also, and my annoyance returned.

"You dismissed our dear friend Ashington very quickly when you heard me coming," I remarked in no very amiable tone.

Tiel looked at me gravely.

"Belke," he said, "you might quite well have done serious mischief by showing your dislike for Ashington so palpably the other day. Even a man of that sort has feelings. I have soothed them, I am glad to say, but he was not very anxious to meet you again."

"So much the better!" said I. "Traitors are not the usual company a German officer keeps."

"Many of us have to mix with strange company nowadays, Mr Belke," said Eileen.

Her sparkling eye and her grave smile disarmed me instantly. I felt suddenly conscious I was not playing a very judicious part, or showing myself perhaps to great advantage. So I bade them both good-night and returned to my room.

But it was not to go to bed. For two mortal hours I paced my floor, and thought and thought, but not about any problem of the war. I kept hearing

Tiel's "Well," spoken in that hatefully intimate way, and then remembering that those two were alone – all night! – in the front part of the house, far out of sound or reach of me. I did not doubt Eileen for an instant, but that calm, cool, cosmopolitan adventurer, who could knock an unsuspecting clergyman on the head and throw him over a cliff, and then tell the story with a smile, – what was he not capable of?

Again and again I asked myself why it concerned me. This was a girl I had only known for hours. But her smile was the last thing I saw before I fell asleep at length about three o'clock in the morning.

VIII. – THE DECISION.

IN THE MORNING I came down to breakfast without asking anybody's leave, and I looked at those two very hard. To see Eileen fresh and calm and smiling gave me the most intense relief, while, as for Tiel, he looked as cool and imperturbable as he always did – and I cannot put it stronger than that, for nothing more cool and imperturbable than Tiel ever breathed. In fact it could not have breathed, for it would have had to be a graven image.

He looked at me critically, but all he said was–

"If it wasn't too wet for your nice uniform, Belke, we might have had breakfast on the lawn."

"You are afraid some one may come and look in at this window?" I asked.

"On the whole there is rather more risk of that than of someone climbing up to look in at your bedroom window," said he.

"You think a great deal of risks," I observed. "Yes," said he. "I am a nervous man."

Eileen laughed merrily, and I could not but confess that for once he had scored. I resolved not to give him the chance again. He then proceeded to draw the table towards one end of the room, pulled the nearest curtain part way across, and then locked the front door. But I made no comments this time.

At breakfast Eileen acted as hostess, and so charming and natural was she that the little cloud seemed to blow over, and we all three discussed our coming plan of attack on the fleet fully and quite freely. Tiel made several suggestions, which he said he had been discussing with Ashington, and, as they seemed extremely sound, I made notes of them and promised to lay them before Wiedermann.

When we had finished and had a smoke, Tiel rose and said he must go out "on parish business." I asked him what he meant, and learned to my amusement that in his capacity of the Rev. Alexander Burnett he had to attend a meeting of what he called the "kirk-session." We both laughed, and wished him good luck, and then before he left he said–

"You had better get back to your room, Belke. Remember we are here on *business.*"

And with that he put on his black felt hat, and bade us lock the front door after him, and if anybody called, explain that it was to keep the wind from shaking it. I must say he thought of these small points very thoroughly.

The suggestion in his last words that I was placing something else before my duty stung me a little. I was not going to let Tiel see that they had any effect, but as soon as he had gone I rose and said to Eileen–

"It is quite clear that I ought to return to my room. I have notes to write up, and several things to do before to-night."·

"Then you are really going to leave us to-night?" said she; "I am very sorry."

So was I. Indeed, the thought of leaving her – probably for ever – would have been bitter enough in any case, but to leave her alone with Tiel was maddening. It had troubled me greatly last night, yet the thought of remaining was one I did not really care to face.

"I fear I must," I replied, in a voice which must have revealed something of what I felt.

"Tiel told me you absolutely refused to listen to him when he wished you to remain."

"Oh no!" I cried. "That is putting it far too strongly."

I offered to put the case to Commander Wiedermann, and then Tiel at once assumed I was going to leave him, and told me to say no more about it."

"Really! That is somewhat extraordinary!" she exclaimed in rather a low voice, as though she were much struck with this. She had been standing, and she sat as she spoke. I felt that she wished to go further into this matter, and I sat down again too.

"What is extraordinary about it?" I asked.

"Do you mean to say that Tiel didn't press you?"

"No," I said.

"Mr Belke," she said earnestly, "I know enough of the orders under which we are acting and the plans that Tiel has got to further, to be quite certain that you were intended to stay and assist him. It is *most* important."

"You are quite sure of this?"

"Absolutely."

"Then why did Tiel give up trying to persuade me so readily? Why didn't he try to use more authority?"

"I wonder," she said in a musing tone, and yet I could see from her eye that she had an idea.

"You know!" I exclaimed. "Tell me what is in your mind!"

Already I guessed, but I dared not put it into words.

"It is difficult to guess Tiel's motives – exactly," she said rather slowly.

I felt I had to say it outright.

"Are you his motive?" I demanded.

She looked at me quickly, but quite candidly.

"I scarcely like to say – or even think such a thing, but –"

She broke off, and I finished her sentence for her.

"But you know he admires you, and is not the man to stick at anything in order to get what he wants."

"Ah! Don't be unjust to him," she answered; and then in a different voice added, "But to think of his letting you go like that!"

"So it was to get rid of me, and have you alone here with him?"

"He must have had some motive," she admitted, "for you *ought* to stay."

"I shall stay!" I said.

She gave me her brightest smile.

"Really? Oh, how good of you! Or rather – how brave of you, for it is certainly running a risk."

If I had been decided before, I was doubly decided now.

"It is not the German navy's way to fear risks," I said. "It is my duty to stay – for two reasons – and I am going to stay!"

"And Commander Wiedermann?"

"I shall simply tell him I am under higher orders, given me by Herr Tiel."

"If you added that there is a second plan directed against the British navy, and that you are needed to advise on the details, it might help to convince Commander Wiedermann how essential your presence here is," she suggested.

"Yes," I agreed, "it would be well to mention that."

"Also," she said, "you would require to have all the details of this first plan so fully written out that he would not need to keep you to explain anything."

"You think of everything!" I cried with an admiration I made no pretence of concealing. "I shall go now and set to work."

"Do!" she cried, "and when Tiel comes in I shall tell him you are going to stay. I wonder what he will say!"

"I wonder too," said I. "But do you care what he says?"

"No," she replied, "because of course he won't say it. He will only think."

"Let him think!" I laughed.

I went back to my room in a strange state of exhilaration for a man who had just decided to forgo the thing he had most looked forward to, and run a horrible risk instead. For I felt in my bones that uniform or no uniform I should be shot if I were caught. I put little trust in English justice or clemency. But, as I said before, when I am obstinate, I am very obstinate; and I was firmly resolved that if Wiedermann wanted me back on board to-night, he would have to call a guard and carry me! However, acting on Eileen's suggestions, I had little doubt I should convince him. And thereupon I set to work on my notes. By evening I had everything so fully written out and so clearly explained that I felt I could say with a clear conscience that even my own presence at a council of war could add no further information.

In the course of the day I had a talk with Tiel, and, just as Eileen had anticipated, he left one to guess at what was in his mind. He certainly professed to be glad I had changed my mind, and he thanked me with every appearance of cordiality.

"You are doing the right thing, Belke," he said. "And, let me tell you, I appreciate your courage."

There was a ring of evident sincerity in his voice as he said this, and whatever I might think of the man's moral character, a compliment from Tiel on one's courage was not a thing to despise.

In the late afternoon he set out to obtain a motor-car for the evening's expedition, but through what ingenious machinery of lies he got it, I was too busy to inquire.

Finally, about ten o'clock at night we sat down to a little supper, my pockets bulging with my notes, and my cyclist's overalls lying ready to be donned once more.

IX. – ON THE SHORE.

SOON after eleven o'clock two dark figures slipped unostentatiously out of the back door, and a moment later a third followed them. My heart leapt with joy and surprise at the sight of it, and Tiel stopped and turned.

"What's the matter?" he asked. "I'm coming too," said Eileen.

"Why?" he demanded in that tone of his which seemed to call upon the questioned to answer with exceeding accuracy.

"Because I'd like a drive," she answered, with a woman's confidence that her reason is good enough for anybody.

"As you please," he said, drily and with unfathomable calm; and then he turned again, and in a voice that betrayed his interest in her, asked, "What have you got on?"

"Quite enough, thank you."

"You are sure? I've lent my spare coat to Belke, but I can get another rug."

"I am quite sure," she smiled.

More than ever I felt glad I was staying beside her.

Tiel sat in front and drove, and Eileen and I got in behind. He offered no objection to this arrangement, though as she seated herself while he was starting the engine, he was certainly not given much choice. And then with a deep purr we rolled off into the night.

There would be no moon till getting on towards morning, but the rain had luckily ceased and the wind fallen, and overhead the stars were everywhere breaking through the last wisps of cloud. Already they gave light enough to distinguish sea from land quite plainly, and very soon they faintly lit the whole wide treeless countryside. The car was a good one, however Tiel had come by it, and the engine was pulling well, and we swept along the lonely roads at a great pace, one bare telegraph post after another flitting swiftly out of the gloom ahead into the gloom behind, and the night air rushing against our faces. At first I looked round me and recognised some features of the way we had come, the steep hill, and the sound that led to the western ocean, and the dark mass of hills beyond, but very soon my thoughts and my eyes alike had ceased to wander out of the car.

We said little, just enough to serve as an excuse for my looking constantly at her profile, and, the longer I looked, admiring the more every line and every curve. All at once she leaned towards me and said in a low beseeching voice–

"You will come back, won't you?"

"I swear it!" I answered fervently, and to give force to my oath I gently took her hand and pressed it. If it did not return the pressure, it at least did not shrink from my clasp. And for the rest of the way I sat holding it.

Presently I in turn leaned towards her and whispered–

"One thing I have been wondering. Should I take Tiel with me to see Wiedermann? It might perhaps be expected."

"No!" she replied emphatically.

"You feel sure?"

For reply she very gently pressed my hand at last. So confident did I feel of her sure judgment that I considered that question settled.

"By the way," she said in a moment, "I think perhaps it might be advisable to say nothing to Commander Wiedermann about me. It is quite unnecessary, and he – well, some men are always suspicious if they think there is a woman in the case. Of course I admit they sometimes have enough excuse, but – what do you think?"

"I agree with you entirely," I said emphatically.

I know Wiedermann very intimately, and had been divided in mind whether I should drop a little hint that there were consolations, or whether I had better not. Now I saw quite clearly I had better not.

"What's that?" said Eileen in a moment.

It was a tall gaunt monolith close to the roadside, and then, looking round, I saw a loch on the other side, and remembered the spot with a start. It was close by here that my cycle had broken down, and we were almost at the end of our drive. Round the corner we swung, straight for the sea, until we stopped where the road ended at the edge of the links.

I gave Eileen's hand one last swift pressure, and jumped out. "We shall wait for you here," said Tiel in a low voice, "but don't be longer than you can help. Remember my nerves!"

He spoke so cheerily and genially, that for the moment I liked him again. In fact, if it had not been for Eileen, and his love of mystery, there was much that was very attractive in Tiel. As I set out on my solitary walk down to the shore, I suddenly wondered what made him so cheerful and bright at this particular moment, for it did not strike me as an exhilarating occasion. And then I was reminded of the man I had known most like Tiel, a captain I once served under, who was silence and calmness itself at most times, but grew strangely genial on critical occasions – a heaven-sent gift. But from Tiel's point of view, what was critical about this moment? The risk he ran at this hour in such an isolated spot was almost negligible, and as to the other circumstances, did it matter much to him whether I stayed or changed my mind and went away? I could scarcely believe it.

I kept along by the side of the sandy track, just as I had done before, only this time I did not lose it. The rolling hummocky links were a little darker, but the stars shone in myriads, bright and clear as a winter's night, and I could see my way well enough. As I advanced, I smelt the same pungent seaweed odour, and heard the same gulls crying, disturbed (I hoped) by the same monster in the waters. Fortunately the storm had blown from the south-east, and the sea in this westward-facing bay heaved quietly, reflecting the radiance of the stars. It was another perfect night for our purpose.

I reached the shore and turned to the left along the rising circumference of the bay, looking hard into the night as I went. Something dark lay on the water, I felt certain of it, and presently something else dark and upright loomed ahead. A moment later I had grasped Wiedermann by the hand. He spoke but a word of cordial greeting, and then turned to descend to the boat.

"We'll get aboard before we talk," said he.

The difficult moment had come. Frankly, I had dreaded it a little, but it had to be faced and got over.

"I am not coming aboard to-night, sir," I replied, He turned and stared at me.

"Haven't you settled anything?" he demanded.

"Something," I said, "but there is more to be done."

I told him then concisely and clearly what we had arranged, and handed him the chart and all my notes. That he was honestly delighted with my news, and satisfied with my own performance, there could be no doubt. He shook me warmly by the hand and said–

"Splendid, Belke! I knew we could count on you! It's lucky you have a chest broad enough to hold all your decorations! For you will get them – never doubt it. But what is all this about staying on shore? What else are you needed for? And who the devil has given you such orders?"

"Herr Tiel," I said. "I was placed under his orders, as you will remember, sir."

"But what does he want you for? And how long does he imagine the British are going to let you stay in this house of yours unsuspected? They are not idiots! It seems to me you have been extraordinarily lucky to have escaped detection so far. Surely you are not going to risk a longer stay?"

"If it is my duty I must run the risk."

"But is it your duty? I am just wondering, Belke, whether I can spare you, with this attack coming on, and whether I ought to override Herr Tiel's orders and damn the consequences!"

I knew his independence and resolution, but just at that moment there passed before my mind's eye such a distinct, sweet picture of Eileen, that I was filled with a resolution and independence even greater than his.

"If it were not my duty, sir," I said firmly, "clearly and strongly pointed out by Herr Tiel, I should never dream of asking you to spare me for a little longer."

"He was then very clear and strong on the question?"

"Extremely."

"And this other scheme of his – do you feel yourself that it is feasible enough to justify you in leaving your ship and running such a terrible risk? Remember, you will be a man lost to Germany!"

I have put down exactly what he said, though it convicts me of having departed a little from the truth when I answered–

"Yes, it will justify the risk."

After all, I had confidence enough in Tiel's abilities to feel sure that I was really justified in saying this; but I determined to press him for some details of his plans tomorrow.

Wiedermann stood silent for a moment; then he held out his hand and said in a sad voice–

"Good-bye! But my mind misgives me. I fear we may never meet again."

"That is nonsense, sir!" I cried as cheerfully as I could. "We shall meet again very soon. And if you wish something to cheer you, just study those plans!"

And so we parted, he descending the bank without another word, and I setting out along the path that by now was beginning to feel quite familiar. I did not even pause to look back this time. My boats were burnt and I felt it was better to hurry on without dwelling longer on the parting. Besides, there was a meeting awaiting me.

When I reached the end of the road, I found that Tiel had been spending the time in turning the car, and now he and Eileen stood beside it, but apparently not conversing.

"All right?" he asked.

"Yes," I said. "I met Wiedermann and gave him all the plans."

He merely nodded and went to start the engine. Again I was forcibly reminded of my old captain, and the way in which he became calmer and more silent than ever the moment the crisis was passed. But surely this crisis had been mine and not his! Anyhow, I felt a singularly strong sense of reaction and seated myself beside Eileen without a word. We had gone for a little way on our homeward road before either of us spoke, and then it was to exchange some quite ordinary remark I put out my hand gently, but hers was nowhere to be found, and this increased my depression. I fell very silent, and then suddenly, when we were nearly back, I exclaimed–

"I wonder whether you are really glad that I returned?"

"Very!" she said, and there was such deep sincerity in her voice that the cloud began to lift at once.

Yet I was not in high spirits when I re-entered my familiar room.

PART IV.

LIEUTENANT VON BELKE'S NARRATIVE CONCLUDED.

I. – WEDNESDAY.

I WOKE on Wednesday morning with an outlook so changed that I felt as if some magician must have altered my nature. Theoretically I had taken a momentous and dangerous decision at the call of duty, and all my energies ought to have concentrated on the task of carrying it through safely, thoroughly, and warily. I had need of more caution than ever, and of the most constant vigilance – both for the sake of my skin and my country. As a matter of fact I was possessed with the recklessness of a man drifting on a plank down a rapid, where taking thought will not serve him an iota. In vain I preached theoretical caution to myself – exactly how vainly may be judged by my first performance in the morning when I found myself alone with Eileen in the parlour. She suggested that for my own sake I had better be getting back to my room.

"Will you come and sit there with me?" I asked.

"I may pay a call upon you perhaps."

"After hours of loneliness! And then leave me lonelier than ever! No, thank you, I shall stay down here."

"In your uniform?" she asked, opening her eyes a little. "No, no, Mr Belke!"

"Well then, get me a suit of mufti!"

She looked at me hard.

"You will really run that risk?"

"It is now worth it," I said with meaning.

She looked away, and for a moment I thought she was pained – not displeased, I am sure, but as if something had given her a pang of sorrow. Then the look passed, and she cried–

"Well, if Tiel agrees!"

"Tiel be hanged! I don't care what he says!"

She began to smile.

"Do you propose to wear my clothes?" she inquired.

"Yours!" I exclaimed.

"Otherwise," she continued, "you must persuade Tiel to agree, for it is only he who can provide you with a suit of mufti."

Presently Tiel came in and I put the demand to him at once. He looked a little surprised, but, somewhat to my surprise, raised no serious objections. His motives are hard to fathom, but I cannot help suspecting that despite his air of self-confidence and authority, he has an instinctive respect for an officer and acknowledges in his heart that I am really his superior.

"You mustn't go outside the house, of course," he said, "and if by any evil chance any visitor were to come in unexpectedly, you must have some kind of a story ready."

"Have you had many visitors yet?" I asked with a touch of sarcasm.

"You never know your luck." said he, "and I believe in guarding against all chances. If you are surprised, please remember that your name is Mr Wilson."

"Wilson?" I said with some disgust. "Am I named in honour of that swine in America?"

"You are named Wilson," said he, "because it is very like Watson and Williams and several other common names. The less conspicuous and more easily forgotten a name one takes, the better."

There is no doubt about the thoroughness of the man and the cunning with which he lays even the smallest plans, and though I was a little contemptuous of his finesse at the moment, I must confess I was thankful enough for it not so very long afterwards.

"As for your business," added Tiel, "you are a Government inspector."

" Of what?" I asked.

"If you are asked, look deep and say nothing," said he. "The islands are full of people on what they call in the Navy 'hush' jobs."

"You seem pretty intimately acquainted with the British Navy down to its slang," I observed.

My nerves were perhaps a little strained this morning, and I meant by this to make a sarcastic allusion to the kind of blackguards he dealt with – such as Ashington. I glanced at Eileen as I spoke, and I was surprised to see a sudden look, almost of alarm, in her eye. It was turned on Tiel, but he appeared absolutely indifferent. I presumed she feared he might take offence and make a row, but she need not have worried. It would take a very pointed insult to rouse that calculating machine.

"Can you get a suit of mufti for me?" I inquired.

"I'll look out one presently," said he.

"I presume you keep a few disguises!" I added.

"A few," said he with one of his brief smiles. "You had better go up to your room in the meantime, and I'll bring it to you."

I fumed at the idea of any delay, and as I went to the door I said–

"Don't be long about it, please!"

More and more the thought of leaving those two alone together, even for a short while, filled me with angry uneasiness, and I paced my bedroom floor impatiently enough. Judge then of my relief and delight when within a few minutes Eileen knocked at my door and said–

"I have come to pay you a morning call if I may."

I began to wish then that Herr Tiel would spend an hour or two in looking out clothes for me, and as a matter of fact he did. Eileen explained that he had said he must do some errand in his capacity as parish minister, but what the mystery-monger was really about, Heaven knows!

"Now," said I to Eileen, when we were seated and I had lit a cigarette, "I want to ask you something about this new scheme that we three are embarked upon."

She began to shake her head at once.

"I am very much in the dark," said she. "Tiel tells me as little as he tells you."

"You must surely know one thing. What is your own part in it? Why were you brought into the islands? Such risks are not run for nothing."

"What is a woman's part in such a plan usually?" she asked in a quiet voice.

I was a little taken aback. It was not exactly pleasant to think of – in connection with Eileen.

"I believe they sometimes act as decoys," I said bluntly.

She merely nodded.

"Then that is your *rôle*?"

"I presume so," she said frankly.

"Who are you going to decoy?" I asked, and I felt that my voice was harsh.

"Ask Herr Tiel," she answered.

"Not that gross brute Ashington surely!"

She shook her head emphatically, and I felt a little relieved.

"You have seen for yourself that he needs no further decoying," she said.

"Then it must be some even higher game you're to be flown at."

"I wonder!" she said, and smiled a little. I hated to see her smile.

"I don't like to think of you doing this," I exclaimed suddenly.

"Not even for Germany?" she asked.

I was silenced, but my blood continued to boil at the thought of what might not be asked of her.

"Would you go to any lengths?" I asked abruptly.

"For my country I would, to any lengths!" she answered proudly.

Again I felt rebuked, yet still more savage at the thought. "You would even become some British Admiral's mistress?" I asked in a low voice.

Her colour suddenly rose, and for an instant she seemed to start. Then in rather a cool voice she said–

"Perhaps we are thinking of rather different things."

And with that she changed the subject, nor could I induce her to return to it. I admit frankly I was a little puzzled. Her reception of my question, perfectly honestly put, had been curiously unlike the candour I should have expected in a girl of her strange profession, especially considering her defiance of all conventionalities in living alone here with two men, and sitting at this moment in the room of one of them. I respected her the more for her hint of affronted dignity. Yet I confess I felt bewildered.

How long we had talked I know not, when at last Tiel appeared, bringing a very presentable tweed suit, and then they both left me, and I did the one thing I had so firmly resolved not to do. I discarded my uniform with what protection it gave me, and made myself liable to be shot without question or doubt. Yet my only feeling was gladness that I need no longer stay cooped up in my room while those two spent their hours together downstairs.

That afternoon, when we were all three together, I asked Tiel for some definite information regarding his scheme, and we had a long, and I must say a very interesting, talk. The details of this plan it would scarcely be safe to put down on paper at present. Or rather, I should say, the outline of it, for we have scarcely reached the stage of details yet. It is a bold scheme, as was only to be expected of Tiel, and necessitated going very thoroughly into the relative naval strengths of Germany and Britain, so that most of the time for the rest of the day was taken up with a discussion of facts and figures. And through it all Eileen sat listening. I wonder if such a talk ever before had such a charming background?

Now at last I am in my room, writing this narrative up to this very point. It is long past midnight, but sleep is keeping very far away from me. The weather has changed to a steady drizzle of rain. Outside, the night is black as pitch, and mild and windless. It may partly be this close damp air that drives sleep away, but I know it is something else as well.

I am actually wondering if I can marry her! She must surrender; that is certain, for I have willed it, and what a German wills with all his soul takes place. It must! As to her heart, I feel sure that her kindness means what a woman's kindness always means – that a man has only to persevere. But marriage?

I shall never meet another woman like her; that is certain! Yet an adventuress, a paid agent of the Secret Service, marrying a von Belke – is it quite conceivable? On the whole I think *no*. But we can be very happy without that! I never loved a woman so much before – that is my last word for the night !

II. – THURSDAY.

Friday morning (very early). – The events of yesterday and last night have left me with more to think about than I seem to have wits to think with. Mein Gott, if I could see daylight through everything! What is ahead, Heaven knows, but here is what is behind.

Yesterday morning passed as the afternoon before had passed, in further discussion of naval statistics with Tiel – with a background of Eileen. Then we had lunch, and soon afterwards Tiel put on an oilskin coat and went out. A thin fine drizzle still filled the air, drifting in clouds before a rising wind and blotting out the view of the sea almost completely. Behind it the ships were doing we knew not what; certainly they were not firing, but we could see nothing of them at all.

A little later Eileen insisted on putting on a waterproof and going out too. As the minister's sister she had to visit a farm, she said. I believed her, of course, though I had ceased to pay much attention to Tiel's statements as to his movements. I knew that he knew his own business thoroughly, and I had ceased to mind if he had not the courtesy to take me into his confidence. After all, if I come safely out of this business, I am not likely to meet such as Tiel again!

Left to myself, I picked up a book and had been reading for about a quarter of an hour when I was conscious of a shadow crossing the window and heard a step on the gravel.

Never doubting that it was either Eileen or Tiel, I still sat reading until I was roused by the sound of voices in the hall, just outside the parlour door. One I recognised as our servant's, the other was a stranger's. I dropped my book and started hastily to my feet, and as I did so I heard the stranger say –

"I tell you I recognise her coat. My good woman, d'ye think I'm blind? I'm coming in to wait for her, I tell you."

The door opened, and a very large stout gentleman appeared, talking over his shoulder as he entered.

"When Miss Holland comes in, tell her Mr Craigie is waiting to see her," said he; and with that he closed the door and became aware of my presence.

For a moment we looked at one another. My visitor, I saw, had a grey beard, a large rosy face, and twinkling blue eyes. He looked harmless enough, but I eyed him very warily, as you can readily believe.

"It's an awful wet day," said he in a most friendly and affable tone.

I agreed that it was detestable.

"It's fine for the crops all the same. The oats is looking very well; do you not think so?"

I perceived that my friend was an agriculturist, and endeavoured to humour him.

"They are looking splendid!" I said with enthusiasm.

He sat down, and we exchanged a few more remarks on the weather and the crops, in the course of which he had filled and lit a pipe and made himself entirely at home.

"Are you staying with the minister?" he inquired presently.

"I am visiting him," I replied evasively.

" I understand Miss Holland's here too," said he, with an extra twinkle in his eye.

I knew, of course, that he must mean Eileen, and I must confess that I was devoured with curiosity.

"She is," I said. "Do you know her? "

" Know her? She was my governess! Has she not told you the joke of how she left me in the lurch?"

It flashed across my mind that it might seem odd if I were to admit that 'Miss Holland' had said nothing about this mysterious adventure.
"Oh yes, she has told us all about it," I replied with assurance.

Mr Craigie laughed heartily at what was evidently a highly humorous recollection .

"I was as near being annoyed at the time as I ever was in my life," said he. "But, man, I've had some proper laughs over it since."

He suddenly grew a trifle graver .

"Mrs Craigie isn't laughing, though. Between ourselves, it's she that's sent me on this errand to-day."

He winked and nodded and relit his pipe, while I endeavoured to see a little light through the extraordinary confusion of ideas which his remarks had caused in my mind.

"Miss Holland came up to the islands as your governess, I understand," I said in as matter of-fact tone as I could compass.

"We got her through a Mrs Armitage in Kensington," said Mr Craigie. "It seemed all right – and mind you, I'm not saying it isn't all right now! Only between you and me, Mr–?"

"Wilson," I said promptly, breathing my thanks to Tiel at the same time.

"You'll be a relation of the minister's too, perhaps?"

"I am on government business," I replied in a suitable tone of grave mystery.

"Damn it, Mr Wilson," exclaimed my friend with surprising energy, "everyone in the country seems to be on government business nowadays – except myself! And I've got to pay their salaries! We're asked in the catechism what's our business in this weary world, and damn it, I can answer that conundrum now! It's just to pay government officials their wages, and build a dozen or two new Dreadnoughts, and send six million peaceable men into the army, and fill a pile of shells with trinitrol-globule-paralysis, or whatever they call the stuff, and all this on the rental of an estate which was just keeping me comfortably in tobacco before this infernal murdering business began! Do you know what I'd do with that Kaiser if I caught him?"

I looked as interested as possible, and begged for information.

"I'd give him my wife and my income, and see how he liked the mess he's landed me in!"

Though Mr Craigie had spoken with considerable vehemence, he had not looked at all fierce, and now his not usually very intellectual face began to assume a thoughtful expression.

"He's an awful fool, yon man!" he observed.

"Which man?" I inquired.

"Billy," said he, and with a gasp I recognised my Emperor in this brief epithet. "It's just astounding to me how he never learns that hot coals will burn his fingers, and water won't run uphill! He's always trying the silliest things."

His eyes suddenly began to twinkle again, and he asked abruptly–

"Why's the Kaiser like my boots?" I gave it up at once.

"Because he'll be sold again soon!" he chuckled. "That's one of my latest, Mr Wilson. I've little to do in these weary times but make riddles to amuse my girls and think of dodges for getting a rise out of my wife. I had her beautifully the other day! We've two sons at the front, you must know, and one of them's called Bob. Well, I got a letter from him, and suddenly I looked awful grave and cried, 'My God, Bob's been blown up '– you should have seen Mrs Craigie jump – 'by his Colonel!' said I, and I tell you she was nearly as put about to find I'd been pulling her leg as if he'd really been blown to smithereens. Women are funny things."

I fear I scarcely laughed as much as he expected at this extraordinary instance of woman's obtuseness, but he did not seem to mind. He was already filling another pipe, and having found an audience, was evidently settling down to an afternoon's conversation – or rather an afternoon's monologue, for it was quite clear he was independent of any assistance from me. I was resolved, however, not to forgo this chance of learning something more about Eileen.

"You were talking about Miss Holland," I said hurriedly, before he had time to get under way again.

"Oh, so I was. And that reminds me I've come here just to make some inquiries about the girl."

Again his blue eyes twinkled furiously.

"Why's Miss Holland like our hall clock?" he inquired. "I may mention by the way that it's always going slow."

Again I gave it up.

"Because you take her hand and get forward! That was one for my wife's benefit. It made her fairly sick!"

"Do you mean," I demanded, "that you were actually in the habit of holding Miss-er-Holland's hand?"

"Oh, no fears. I'm past that game. But Mrs Craigie is a great one for p's and q's and not being what she calls vulgar, and a joke like that is a sure draw. I get her every time with my governess riddles. Here's a good one now – Why's a pretty governess like a – "

In spite of the need for caution, my impatience was fast overcoming me.

"Then you have been sent by Mrs Craigie to make inquiries about Miss Holland?" I interrupted a trifle brusquely.

Mr Craigie seemed at least to have the merit of not taking offence readily.

"That's the idea," he agreed. "You see, it's this way: my wife's been at me ever since our governess bolted, as she calls it. Well now, what's the good in making inquiries about a thing that's happened and finished and come to an end? If it was a case of engaging another governess, that's a different story. I'd take care not to have any German spies next time!"

" German spies!" I exclaimed, with I hope well-simulated horror; "you don't mean to suspect Miss Holland of *that* surely!"

"Oh, 'German Spy' is just a kind of term nowadays for anyone you don't know all about," said Mr Craigie easily. "Every one you haven't seen before is a German Spy. I spotted five myself in my own parish at the beginning of the war, and Mrs Craigie wrote straight off to the Naval Authorities and reported them all."

"And were they actually spies?" I asked a trifle uncomfortably.

"Not one of them!" laughed he. "The nearest approach was a tinker who'd had German measles! Ha, ha! It's no good my wife reporting any more spies, and I just reminded her of that whenever she worried me, and pulled her leg a bit about me and Miss Holland being in the game together, and so it was all right till she got wind of a girl who was the image of the disappearing governess being here at the manse as Mr Burnett's sister, and then there was simply no quieting her till I'd taken the car and run over to see what there was in the story. Mind you, I didn't think there was a word of truth in it myself; but when I'd got here, by Jingo, there I saw Miss Holland's tweed coat in the hall! Now that's a funny kettle of fish, isn't it?"

I didn't say so, but I had to admit that he was not so very far wrong. The audacity of the performance was quite worthy of Tiel, but its utter recklessness seemed not in the least like him. Had the vanishing governess's employer been anyone less easy-going than Mr Craigie, how readily our whole scheme might have been wrecked! Even as it was, I saw detection staring me straight in the face. However, I put on as cool and composed a face as I could.

"I understood that Miss Holland's brother had written to you about it," I said brazenly.

"Oh! he is really her brother, is he?" said he, looking at me very knowingly.

"Certainly."

"He being Burnett and she Holland, eh?"

"You have heard of half-brothers, haven't you?" I inquired with a condescending smile.

"Oh, I have heard of them," winked Mr Craigie as good-humouredly as ever; "only I never happened to have heard before of half-sisters running away from a situation they'd taken without a word of warning, just whenever their half-brothers whistled."

"Did Mr Burnett whistle?" I inquired, with (I hope) an air of calm and slightly superior amusement.

"Someone sent her a wire, and I presume it was Mr Burnett," said he. "By Jingo!"

He stopped suddenly with an air as nearly approaching excitement as was conceivable in such a gentleman.

"What's the matter?" I asked a trifle anxiously.

"One might get a good one about how to make a governess explode, the answer being 'Burn it!' By Jove, I must think that out."

Before I could recover from my amazement at this extraordinary attitude, he had suddenly resumed his shrewd quizzical look.

"Are you an old friend of Mr Burnett?" he inquired. "Oh, not very," I said carelessly.

"Then perhaps you'll not be offended by my saying that he seems a rum kind of bird," he said confidentially.

"In what way?"

"Well, coming up here just for a Sunday to preach a sermon, and then not preaching it, but staying on as if he'd taken a lease of the manse – him and his twelve-twenty-fourths of a sister!"

"But," I stammered, before I could think what I was saying, "I thought he did preach last Sunday!"

"Not him! Oh, people are talking a lot about it."

This revelation left me absolutely speechless. Tiel had told me distinctly and deliberately that he had gone through the farce of preaching last Sunday – and now I learned that this was a lie. What was worse, he had assured me that he was causing no comment, and I now was told that people were "talking." Coming straight on top of my discovery of his reckless conduct of Eileen's affair, what was I to think of him?

It was at this black moment that Tiel and Eileen entered the room. My heart stood still for an instant at the thought that, in their first surprise, something might be disclosed or some slip made by one of us. But the next instant I saw that they had learned who was here and were perfectly prepared.

"How do you do, Mr Craigie!" cried Eileen radiantly.

Mr Craigie seemed distinctly taken aback by the absence of all signs of guilt or confusion.

"I'm keeping as well as I can, thank you, considering my anxiety," said he.

"About my sister, sir?" inquired Tiel with his most brazen effrontery, coming forward and smiling cordially. "Surely you got my letter? "

I started. The man clearly had been at the key-hole during the latter part of our conversation, or he could hardly have made this remark fit so well into what I had said.

"I'm afraid I didn't."

"Tut, tut!" said Tiel, with a marvellously well-assumed air of annoyance. "The local posts seem to have become utterly disorganised. Apparently they pay no attention to civilian letters at all."

"You're right there," replied Mr Craigie with feeling. "The only use we are for is just to be taxed."

"What must you think of us?" cried Eileen, whose acting was fully the equal of Tiel's. "However, my brother will explain everything now."

"Yes," said Tiel; "if Mr Craigie happens to be going –and I'm afraid we've kept him very late already – I'll tell him all about it as we walk back to his car."

He gave Mr Craigie a confidential glance as though to indicate that he had something private for his ear. Our visitor, on his part, was obviously reluctant to leave an audience of three, especially as it included his admired governess; but Tiel handled the situation with quite extraordinary urbanity and skill. He managed to open the door and all but pushed Mr Craigie out of the room, without a hint of inhospitality, and solely as though he were seeking only his convenience. I could scarcely believe that this was the man who had made at least two fatal mistakes – mistakes, at all events, which had an ominously fatal appearance.

When Mr Craigie had wished us both a very friendly good-bye and the door had closed behind him, I turned instantly to Eileen and cried, perhaps more hotly than politely–

"Well, I have been nicely deceived!"

"By whom?" she asked quietly.

"By you a little and by Tiel very much!"

"How have I deceived you?"

I looked at her a trifle foolishly. After all, I ought to have realised that she must have had some curious adventure in getting into the islands. She had never told me she hadn't and now I had merely found out what it was.

"You never told me about your governess adventure – or Mr Craigie – or that you were called Holland," I said rather lamely.

She merely laughed.

"You never asked me about my adventures, or I should have. They were not very discreditable after all."

"Well, anyhow," I said, "Tiel has deceived me grossly, and I am going to wring an explanation out of him! "

She laid her hand beseechingly on my arm.

"Don't quarrel with him!" she said earnestly. "It will do no good. We may think what we like of some of the things he does, but we have got to trust him!"

"Trust him! But how can I? He told me he preached last Sunday, – I find it was a lie. He said nobody in the parish suspected anything, – in consequence of his not preaching, I find they are all 'talking.' He mismanaged your coming here so badly that if old Craigie weren't next door to an imbecile we should all have been arrested days ago. How can I trust him now?"

"Say nothing to him now," she said in a low voice.

"Wait till to-morrow! I think he will tell you then very frankly."

There was something so significant and yet beseeching in her voice that I consented, though not very graciously.

"I can hardly picture Herr Tiel being very 'frank'!" I replied. "But if you ask me –"

I bowed my obedience, and then catching up her hand pressed it to my lips, saying–

"I trust you absolutely!"

When I looked up I caught a look in her eye that I could make nothing of at all. It was beyond question very kind, yet there seemed to be something sorrowful too. It made her look so ravishing that I think I would have taken her in my arms there and then, had not Tiel returned at that moment.

"Well," asked Eileen, "what did you tell Mr Craigie?"

"I said that you were secretly married to Mr Wilson, whose parents would cut him off without a penny if they suspected the entanglement, and this was the only plan by which you could spend a few days together. Of course, I swore him to secrecy."

For a moment I hesitated whether to resent this liberty, or to feel a little pleased, or to be amused. Eileen laughed gaily, and so I laughed too. And that was the end (so far) of my afternoon adventure.

III. – THURSDAY NIGHT.

I WENT up to my room early in the evening. Eileen had been very silent, and about nine o'clock she bade us good-night and left us. To sit alone with Tiel, feeling as I did and yet bound by a promise not to upbraid him, was intolerable, and so I left the parlour a few minutes after she did. As I went down the passage to the back, my way lit only by the candle I was carrying, I was struck with a sound I had heard in that house before, only never so loudly. It was the droning of the wind through the crevices of some door, and the whining melancholy note in the stillness of that house of divided plotters and confidences withheld, die nothing to raise my spirits.

When I reached my room I realised what had caused the droning. The wind had changed to a new quarter, and as another consequence my chimney was smoking badly and the room was filled with a pungent blue cloud. It is curious how events arise as consequences of trifling and utterly different circumstances. I tried opening my door and then my window, but still the fire smoked and the cloud refused to disperse. Then I had an inspiration. I have mentioned a large cupboard. It was so large as almost to be a minute room, and I remembered that it had a skylight in its sloping roof. I opened this, and as the room at once began to clear, I left it open.

And then I paced the floor and smoked and thought.

What was to be made of these very disquieting events? Clearly Tiel was either a much less capable and clever man than he was reputed – a bit of a fraud in fact – or else he was carrying his fondness for mystery and for suddenly springing brilliant surprises, like conjuring tricks, upon people, to the most extreme lengths. If he were really carrying out a cunning deliberate policy in not preaching last Sunday, good and well, but it was intolerable that he should have deceived me about it. It seemed quite a feasible theory to suppose that he had got out of conducting the service on some excuse in order that he might be asked to stay longer and preach next Sunday instead. But then he had deliberately told me he had preached, and that the people had been so pleased that they had invited him to preach again. It sounded like a schoolboy's boastfulness!

Of course if he were the sort of man who would (like myself) have drawn the line at conducting a bogus religious service, I could quite well understand his getting out of it somehow. But when I remembered his tale of the murder of the real Mr Burnett, I dismissed that hypothesis. Besides, why deceive me in any case? I daresay I should have felt a little anxious as to the result if he had evaded the duty he had professed to come up and perform, but would he care twopence about that? I did not believe it.

And then his method of getting Eileen into the islands, though ingenious enough (if not very original), had been marred by the most inconceivable recklessness. Surely some better scheme could have been devised for getting her out of the Craigies' house than a sudden flight without a word of explanation – and a flight, moreover, to another house in the same island where gossip would certainly spread in the course of a very few days. Of course Mr Craigie's extraordinary character gave the scheme a chance it never deserved, but was Tiel really so diabolically clever that he actually counted on that? How could he have known so much of Craigie's character? Indeed, that explanation was inconceivable.

And then again, why had Eileen consented to such a wild plan? That neither of them should have realised its drawbacks seemed quite extraordinary. There must be some deep cunning about it that escaped me altogether. If it were not so, we were lost indeed! And so I resolved to believe that there was more wisdom in the scheme than I realised, and simply leave it at that.

Thereupon I sat down and wrote for an hour or two to keep me from thinking further on the subject, and at last about midnight I resolved to go to bed. The want of fresh air had been troubling me greatly, and it struck me that a safe way of getting a little would be to put my head through the open skylight for a few minutes. It was quite dark in the cupboard, so that no light could escape; and I brought a chair along, stood on it, and looked out, with my head projecting from the midst of the sloping slates, and a beautiful cool breeze refreshing my face.

So cool was the wind that there was evidently north in it, and this was confirmed by the sky, which literally blazed with stars. I could see dimly but pretty distinctly the outbuildings at the back of the house, and the road that led to the highway, and the dark rim of hills beyond. Suddenly I heard the back door gently open, and still as I had stood on my chair before, I became like a statue now. In a moment the figure of Tiel appeared, and from a flash of light I saw that he carried his electric torch. He walked slowly towards the highroad till he came to a low wall that divided the fields at the side, and then from behind the wall up jumped the form of a man, illuminated for an instant by a flash from the torch, and then just distinguishable in the gloom.

I held my breath and waited for the crack of a pistol-shot, gently withdrawing my head a little, and prepared to rush down and take part in the fray. But there was not a sound save a low murmur of voices, far too distant and too hushed for me to catch a syllable of what they were saying. And then after two or three minutes I saw Tiel turn and start to stroll back again. But at that moment my observations ceased, for I stepped hastily down from my chair and stood breathlessly waiting for him to run up to my room.

He was quiet almost as a mouse. I had not heard him pass through the house as he went out, and I barely heard a sound now as he returned. But I heard enough to know that he had gone off to bed, and did not propose to pay me a visit.

"What in Heaven's name did it mean?" I asked myself. A dozen wild and alarming theories flashed through my mind, and then at last I saw a ray of comfort. Perhaps this was only a rendezvous with Ashington, or some subordinate in his pay. It was not a very brilliant ray, for the more I thought over it, the more unlikely it seemed that a rendezvous should take place at that spot and in that inconvenient fashion, when there was nothing to prevent Ashington or his emissary from entering the house by the front door and holding their conversation in the parlour. However, it seemed absolutely the only solution, short of supposing that the house was watched, and so I accepted it for what it was worth in the meantime, and turned into bed.

My sleep was very broken, and in the early morning I felt so wide awake, and my thoughts were so restlessly busy, that I jumped up and resolved to have another peep out of the skylight. Very quietly I climbed on the chair and put my head through again. There was the man, pacing slowly away from me, from the wall towards the highroad! I studied his back closely, and of two things I felt certain: he was not a sailor of any sort-officer or bluejacket – and yet he walked like a drilled man. A tall, square-shouldered fellow, in dark plain clothes, who walks with a short step and a stiff back-what does that suggest? A policeman of some sort – constable or detective, no doubt about that!

At the road he turned, evidently to stroll back again, and down went my head. I did not venture to look out again, nor was there any need. I dressed quickly, and this time put on my uniform. This precaution seemed urgently – and ominously – called for! And then I slipped downstairs, went to the front hall, and up the other stairs, and quietly called "Tiel!" For I confess I was not disposed to sit for two or three hours waiting for information.

At my second cry he appeared at his bedroom door, prompt as usual.

"What's the matter?" he asked.

"Who did you speak to last night?" I asked point-blank.

He looked at me for an instant and then smiled.

"Good heavens, it wasn't you, was it?" he inquired.

"Me!" I exclaimed.

"I wondered how you knew otherwise." I told him briefly.

"And now tell me exactly what happened!" I demanded.

"Certainly," said he quietly. "I went out, as I often do last thing at night, to see that the coast is clear, and this time I found it wasn't. A man jumped up from behind the wall just as you saw."

"Who was he?"

"I can only suspect. I saw him for an instant by the light of my torch, and then it seemed less suspicious to put it out."

"I don't see that," I said.

"I am a cautious man," smiled Tiel, as easily as though the incident had not been of life and death importance.

"And what did he say to you? "I demanded impatiently.

"I spoke to him and asked him what he was doing there."

"What did he say to that?"

"I gave him no chance to answer – because, if the answer was what I feared, he wouldn't make it. I simply told him he would catch cold if he sat there on the grass, and gave him some details about my own misfortune in getting rheumatism through sleeping in damp sheets."

"I see," I said; "you simply tried to bluff him by behaving like an ordinary simple-minded honest clergyman?"

Tiel nodded.

"It was the only thing to do – unless I had shot him there and then. And there might have been more men for all I knew."

"Well," I said, "I can tell you something more about that man. He is patrolling the road at the back at this very moment."

Tiel looked grave enough now.

"It looks as if the house were being watched," he said rather slowly.

"Looks? It *is* being watched!" He thought for a moment.

"Evidently they only suspect so far. They can know nothing, or they wouldn't be content with merely watching. Thank you for telling me. We'll talk about it later."

Still cool as a cucumber he re-entered his room, and I returned to my own.

What can be done? Nothing! I can only sit and wait and keep myself from worrying by writing. I have made up my fire and my door is locked, so that this manuscript will be in flames before anyone can enter, if it comes to the worst. Recalling the words of Tiel a few days ago, I shiver a little to think of what is ahead. Suspicion has *begun*!

IV. – FRIDAY.

THIS is written under very different circumstances – and in a different place. My last words were written with my eyes shut; these are written with them open, but I shall simply tell what happened as calmly as I can. Let the events speak; I shall make no comment in the meanwhile.

On that Friday morning our breakfast was converted into a council of war. We all three discussed the situation gravely and frankly. I felt tempted to say some very bitter words to Tiel, for it seemed to me quite obvious that it was simply his gross mismanagement which had brought us to the edge of this precipice; but I am glad now I refrained. I was at no pains, however, to be over-polite.

"There is nothing to be done in the meanwhile, I'm afraid," said he.

This coolness seemed to me all very well in its proper season, but not at present.

"Yes, there is," I said urgently. "We might get out of this house and look for some other refuge!" He shook his head.

"Not by daylight, if it is being watched."

"Besides," said Eileen, "this is the day we have been waiting for. We don't want to be far away, do we?"

"Personally," I said, "it seems to me that as I cannot be where I ought to be" (and here I looked at Tiel somewhat bitterly), "with my brave comrades in their attack on our enemies, I should much prefer to make for a safer place than this – if one can be found."

"It can't," said Tiel briefly.

And that indeed became more and more obvious the longer we talked it over. Had our house stood in the midst of a wood, or had a kindly fog blown out of the North Sea, we might have made a move. As it was, I had to agree that it would be sheer folly, before nightfall anyhow; and there was nothing for it but waiting.

To add to the painfulness of this ordeal, I found myself obliged to remain in my room, now that I had resumed my uniform. This time it did not need Tiel to bid me take this precaution. In fact, I was amazed to hear him suggesting that I would be just as safe in the parlour. At the time I naturally failed altogether to understand this departure from his usual caution, and I asked him sarcastically if he wished to precipitate a catastrophe.

"We have still a good deal to discuss," said he. "I thought there was nothing more to be said."

"I mean in connection with the other scheme."

"The devil may take the other scheme!" said I, "anyhow till we escape from this trap. What is the good in planning ahead, with the house watched night and day?"

"We only suspect it is watched," said he calmly.

"Suspect!" I cried. "We are not idiots, and why should we pretend to be?"

And so I went up to my room and spent the most miserable and restless day of my life. How slowly the hours passed, no words of mine can give the faintest idea. In my present state of mind writing was impossible, and I tried to distract myself by reading novels; but they were English novels, and every word in them seemed to gall me. I implored Eileen to come and keep me company. She came up once for a little, but the devil seemed to have possessed her, for I felt no sympathy coming from her at all; and when at last I tried to be a little affectionate she first repulsed me, saying it was no time for that, and then she left me. With baffled love added to acute anxiety, you can picture my condition!

For the first part of that horrible day I kept listening for some sign of the police, and now and then looking out from the skylight at the back, but the watcher was no longer visible, and not a fresh step or voice was to be heard in the house. My door stood locked, my fire was blazing, and my papers lay ready to be consumed, and at moments I positively longed to see them blazing and myself arrested, and get it over, yet nothing happened.

In the afternoon the direction of my thoughts began to change as the hour approached when the fleet should sail and my country reap the reward of the enterprise and fidelity which I felt conscious I had shown, and the sacrifice which I feared I should have to make. I began to make brief visits to the parlour to look out of the window and see if I could see any signs of movement in the Armada. And then for the second time I saw Tiel in a genial cheerful humour, and this time there was no doubt of the cause. He too was in a state of tension, and his mind, like mine, was running on the coming drama. In fact, as the afternoon wore on, his thoughts were so entirely wrapped up in this that he frankly talked of nothing else. Was I sure we should have at least four submarines? he asked me; and would they be brought well in and take the risk? Indeed, I never heard him ask so many questions, or appear so pleased as he did when I reassured him on all these points.

As for Eileen, she was quite as excited as either of us, and when Tiel was not asking me questions, she was; until once again prudence drove me back to my room. On one of my visits she gave us some tea, but that is the only meal I remember any of us eating between our early and hurried lunch and the evening when the crash came.

The one thing I looked for as I gazed out of that window was the rising of smoke from the battle-fleet, and at last I saw it. Stream after stream, black or grey, gradually mounted first from one leviathan and then from another, till the air was darkened hundreds of feet above them, and if our flotilla were in such a position that they could look for this sign, they must have seen it. This time I returned to my room with a heart a little lightened.

"I have done my duty," I said to myself, "come what may of it!"

And I do not think that any impartial reader will deny that, so far as my own share of this enterprise was concerned, I had done my very utmost to make it succeed.

The next time I came down my spirits rose higher still, and for the moment I quite forgot the danger in which I stood. The light cruisers, the advance-guard of the fleet, were beginning to move! This time when I went back to my room I forced myself to read two whole chapters of a futile novel before I again took off the lid and peeped in to see how the stew was cooking. The instant I had finished the second chapter I leapt up and opened the door – and then I stood stock-still and listened. A distant sound of voices reached me, and a laugh rang out that was certainly neither Tiel's nor Eileen's.

I locked my door, slipped back again, and prepared to burn my papers; but though I stood over the fire for minute after minute, there was no sound of approaching steps. Very quietly I opened the door and listened once more, and still I heard voices. And thus I lingered and hesitated for more than an hour. By this time the attack had probably been made, and I could stand the suspense no longer, so I went recklessly downstairs, strode along the passage, and opened the parlour door.

Nothing will ever efface the memory of the scene that met my eyes. Tiel, Eileen, and Ashington sat there, the two men each with a whisky-and-soda, and all three seemingly in the most extraordinarily high spirits. It was Ashington's face and voice that suddenly rent the veil from before my eyes. Instead of the morose and surly individual I had met before, he sat there the incarnation of the jovial sailor. He was raising his glass to his lips, and as I entered I heard the words–

"Here's to you again, Robin!"

What had happened I did not clearly grasp in that first instant, but I *felt* I was betrayed. My hand went straight to my revolver pocket, but before I could seize it, Tiel, who sat nearest, leapt up, grasped my wrist, and with the shock of his charge drove me down into a chair. It was done so suddenly that I could not possibly have resisted. Then with a movement like a conjurer he picked the revolver out of my pocket, and said in his infernally cool calm way–

"Please consider yourself a prisoner of war, Mr Belke." Even then I had not grasped the whole truth.

"A prisoner of war!" I exclaimed. "And what the devil are you, Herr Tiel? A traitor?"

"You have got my name a little wrong," said he, with that icy smile of his. "I am Commander Blacklock of the British Navy, so you can surrender either to me or to Captain Phipps, whichever you choose."

"Phipps!" I gasped, for I remembered that as the name of a member of Jellicoe's staff.

"That's me, old man," said the gross person with insufferable familiarity. "The Honourable Thomas Bainbridge Ashington would have a fit if he looked in the glass and saw this mug!"

"Then I understand I am betrayed?" I asked as calmly as I could.

"You're nabbed," said Captain Phipps, with brutal British slang, "and let me tell you that's better than being dead, which you would have been if you'd rejoined your boat."

I could not quite control my feelings. "What has happened?" I cried.

"We've bagged the whole four – just at the very spot on the chart which you and I arranged!" chuckled the great brute. (At this point Lieutenant von Belke's comments become a little too acid for publication, and it has been considered advisable that the narrative should be finished by the Editor.)

PART V.

A FEW CONCLUDING CHAPTERS BY THE EDITOR.

I.-TIEL'S JOURNEY.

FOR the moment the fortitude of the hapless young lieutenant completely broke down when he heard these tidings. It took him a minute to control his voice, and then he said–

"Please give me back my revolver. I give you my word of honour not to use it on any of you three."

Commander Blacklock shook his head.

"I am sorry we can't oblige you," said he.

"Poor old chap," said Phipps with genial sympathy; "it's rotten bad luck on you, I must admit."

These well-meant words seemed only to incense the captive.

"I do not wish your damned sympathy!" he cried.

"Hush, hush! Ladies present," said Phipps soothingly. Von Belke turned a lowering eye on Miss Holland. She had said not a word, and scarcely moved since he came into the room, but her breathing was a little quicker than usual, and her gaze had followed intently each speaker in turn.

"Ach so!" he said; "the decoy is still present. I had forgot."

Blacklock's eye blazed dangerously.

"Mr Belke," he said, "Captain Phipps and I have pleaded very strongly that, in spite of your exceedingly ambiguous position, and the fact that you have not always been wearing uniform, you should not suffer the fate of a spy. But if you make any more remarks like your last, I warn you we shall withdraw this plea."

For the first time Eileen spoke.

"Please do not think it matters to me, Captain Blacklock –" she began.

In a whisper Phipps interrupted her .

"Eye-wash!" he said. "It's the only way to treat a Hun – show him the stick!"

The hint had certainly produced its effect. Von Belke shrugged his shoulders, and merely remarked–

"I am your prisoner. I say nothing more."

"That's distinctly wiser," said Captain Phipps, with a formidable scowl at the captive and a wink at Miss Holland.

For a few moments von Belke kept his word, and sat doggedly silent. Then suddenly he exclaimed–

"But I do not understand all this! How should a German agent be a British officer? My Government knew all about Tiel – I was told to be under his orders – it is impossible you can be he!"

Blacklock turned to the other two.

"I almost think I owe Mr Belke an explanation," he said with a smile.

"Yes," cried Eileen eagerly, "do tell him, and – then he will understand a little better."

Blacklock filled a pipe and leaned his back against the fireplace, a curious mixture of clergyman in his attire and keen professional sailor in his voice and bearing, now that all need for pretence was gone.

"The story I told you of the impersonation and attempted murder of Mr Alexander Burnett," he began, "was simply a repetition of the tale told me by Adolph Tiel at Inverness – where, by the way, he was arrested."

Von Belke started violently.

"So!" he cried. "Then – then you never were Tiel?"

"I am thankful to say I never was, for a more complete scoundrel never existed. He and his friend Schumann actually did knock Mr Burnett on the head, tie a stone to his feet, and pitch him over the cliff. Unfortunately for them, they made a bad job of the knot and the stone came loose. In consequence, Mr Burnett floated long enough to be picked up by a patrol boat, which had seen the whole performance outlined against the sky at the top of the cliff above her. By the time they had brought him back to a certain base, Mr Burnett had revived and was able to tell of his adventure. The affair being in my line, was put into my hands, and it didn't take long to see what the rascals' game was."

"No," commented Phipps; "I suppose you spotted that pretty quick."

"Practically at once. A clergyman on his way here – clothes and passport stolen – left for murdered – chauffeur so like him that the minister noticed the resemblance himself in the instant the man was knocking him down, – what was the inference? Pretty obvious, you'll agree. Well, the first step was simple. The pair had separated; but we got Tiel at Inverness on his way North, and Schumann within twenty-four hours afterwards at Liverpool."

"Good business!" said Phipps. "I hadn't heard about Schumann before."

"Well," continued Blacklock, "I interviewed Mr Tiel, and I found I'd struck just about the worst thing in the way of rascals it has ever been my luck to run up against. He began to bargain at once. If his life was spared he would give me certain very valuable information."

"Mein Gott!" cried Belke. "Did a German actually say that?"

"Tiel belongs to no country," said Blacklock. "He is a cosmopolitan adventurer without patriotism or morals. I told him his skin would be safe if his information really proved valuable; and when I heard his story, I may say that he did save his skin. He gave the whole show away, down to the passwords that were to pass between you when you met."

He suddenly turned to Phipps and smiled.

"It's curious how the idea came to me. I've done a good bit of secret service work myself, and felt in such a funk sometimes that I've realised the temptation to give the show away if I were nailed. Well, as I looked at Tiel, I said to myself, 'There, but for the grace of God, stands Robin Blacklock!' And then suddenly it flashed into my mind that we were really not at all unlike one another – same height, and tin-opener nose, and a few streaks of anno domini in our hair, and so on."

"I know, old thing," said his friend, "it's the wife-poisoning type. You see 'em by the dozen in the Chamber of Horrors."

Their Teutonic captive seemed to wax a little impatient. "What happened then?" he demanded.

"What happened was that I decided to continue Mr Tiel's journey for him. The arrest and so on had lost a day, but I knew that the night of your arrival was left open, and I had to risk it. That splash of salt water on your motor bike, and your resource in dodging pursuit, just saved the situation, and we arrived at the house on the same night."

"So that was why you were late!" exclaimed von Belke. "Fool that I was not to have questioned and suspected!"

"It might have been rather a nasty bunker," admitted Blacklock, "but luckily I got you to lose your temper with me when I reached that delicate part of my story, and you forgot to ask me."

"You always were a tactful fellow, Robin," murmured Phipps.

"Of course," resumed Blacklock, "I was in touch with certain people who advised me what scheme to recommend. My only suggestion was that the officer sent to advise us professionally should be one whose appearance might lead those who did not know him to suspect him capable of treasonable inclinations. My old friend, Captain Phipps – "

"Robin!" roared his old friend, "I read your bloomin' message. You asked for the best-looking officer on the staff, and the one with the nicest manners. Get on with your story! These interludes seemed to perplex their captive considerably.

"You got a pretended traitor? I see," he said gravely.

"Exactly. I tried you first with Ashington of the *Haileybury* – whom I slandered grossly by the way. If you had happened to know him by sight I should have passed on to another captain, till I got one you didn't know. Well, I needn't recall what happened at our council of war, but now we come to rather a – " he hesitated and glanced for an instant at Miss Holland, – "well, rather a delicate point in the story. I think it's only fair to those concerned to tell you pretty fully what happened. I believe I am right in thinking that they would like me to do so."

Again he glanced at the girl, and this time she gave a little assenting nod.

"That night, after you left us, Mr Belke, Captain Phipps and I had a long discussion over a very knotty point. How were we to get you back again here after you had delivered your message to your submarine?"

"I do not see exactly why you wished me to return?" said von Belke.

"There were at least three vital reasons. In the first place some one you spoke to might have known too much about Tiel and have spotted the fraud. Then again, some one might easily have known the real Captain Ashington, and it would be a little difficult to describe Captain Phipps in such a way as to confound him with any one else. Finally, we wished to extract a little more information from you."

Von Belke leapt from his seat with an exclamation.

"What have I not told you!" he cried hoarsely. "Mein Gatt, I had forgotten that! Give me that pistol! Come, give it to me! Why keep me alive?"

"I suppose because it is an English custom," replied Commander Bladdock quietly. "Also, you will be exceedingly glad some day to find yourself still alive. Please sit down and listen. I am anxious to explain this point fully, for a very good reason."

With a groan their captive sat down, but with his head held now between his hands and his eyes cast upon the floor.

"We agreed that at all costs this must be managed, and so I tried my hand at exercising my authority over you. I saw that was going to be no good, and gave it up at once for fear you'd smell a rat. And then I thought of Miss Holland."

Von Belke looked up suddenly.

"Ah!" he cried, "so that is why this lady appeared – this lady I may not call a decoy!"

"That is why," said Blacklock.

II. – THE LADY.

LIEUTENANT VON BELKE looked for a moment at the lady who had enslaved him, but for some reason he averted his gaze rather quickly. Then with an elaborate affectation of sarcastic politeness which served but ill to conceal the pain at his heart and the shock to his pride, he inquired–

"May I be permitted to ask what agency supplies ladies so accomplished at a notice so brief?"

"Providence," said Blacklock promptly and simply. "Miss Holland had never undertaken any such work before, and her name is on the books of no bureau."

"I believe you entirely," said von Belke ironically. "You taught her her trade then, I presume?"

"I did."

The German stared at him.

"Is there really any need to deceive me further?" he inquired.

"I am telling you the simple truth," said Blacklock unruffled. "I had the great good fortune to make Miss Holland's acquaintance on the mail-boat crossing to these islands. She was going to visit Mr Craigie – that intellectual gentleman you met yesterday – under the precise circumstances he described. I noticed Miss Holland the moment she came aboard the boat." He paused for a moment, and then turned to Eileen with a smile. "I have a confession to make to you, Miss Holland, which I may as well get off my chest now. My mind, naturally enough perhaps, was rather running on spies, and when I discovered that you were travelling with a suit-case of German manufacture I had a few minutes' grave suspicion. I now apologise."

Eileen laughed.

"Only a few minutes!" she exclaimed. "It seems to me I got off very easily!"

"That was why I was somewhat persistent in my conversation," he continued, still smiling a little, "but it quickly served the purpose of satisfying me absolutely that my guns were on the wrong target. And so I promptly relieved you of my conversation."

He turned again to von Belke.

"Then, Mr Belke, a very curious thing happened, which one of us may perhaps be pardoned for thinking diabolical and the other providential. Miss Holland happened to have met the real Mr Burnett and bowled me out. And then I had another lucky inspiration. If Miss Holland will pardon me for saying so in her presence, I had already been struck with the fact that she was a young lady of very exceptional looks and brains and character – and, moreover, she knew Germany and she knew German. It occurred to me that in dealing with a young and probably not unimpressionable man such an ally might conceivably come in useful."

"Robin," interrupted his old friend, with his rich laugh, "you are the coldest-blooded brute I ever met!"

"To plot against a man like that!" agreed von Belke with bitter emphasis.

"Oh, I wasn't thinking of you," said Captain Phipps, with a gallant glance at the lady. "However, on you go with your yarn."

"Well, I decided on the spot to take Miss Holland into my confidence – and I should like to say that confidence was never better justified. She seemed inclined to do what she could for her country." Commander Blacklock paused for an instant, and added apologetically, "I am putting it very mildly and very badly, but you know what I mean. She was, in fact, ready to do anything I asked her on receipt of a summons from me. I had thought of her even when talking to Captain Phipps, but I felt a little reluctant to involve her in the business, with all it entailed, unless no other course remained open. And no other course was open. And so I first telegraphed to her and then went over and fetched her. That was how she came to play the part she did, entirely at my request and instigation."

"You – you then told her to – to make me admire her?" asked von Belke in an unsteady voice.

"Frankly I did. Of course it was not for me to teach a lady how to be attractive, but I may say that we rehearsed several of the scenes very carefully indeed, – I mean in connection with such matters as the things you should say to Commander Wiedermann, and so on. Miss Holland placed herself under my orders, and I simply told her what to say. She was in no sense to blame."

"Blame!" cried Captain Phipps. "She deserves all the decorations going!"

"I was trying to look at it from Mr Belke's point of view," said Blacklock, "as I think Miss Holland probably desires."

She gave him a quick, grateful look, and he continued –

"It was I who suggested that she should appear critical of me, and endeavour, as it were, to divide our household into two camps, so that you should feel you were acting against me when you were actually doing what I wished. I tell you this frankly so that you may see who was responsible for the deceit that we were forced to practise."

"Forced!" cried the young lieutenant bitterly. "Who forced you to use a woman? Could you not have deceived me alone?"

"No," said Blacklock candidly, "I couldn't, or I should not have sent for Miss Holland. It was an extremely difficult problem to get you to risk your life, and stand out against your commanding officer's wishes and your own inclinations and your apparent duty, and come back to this house after the whole plan was arranged and every argument seemed to be in favour of your going aboard your boat again. Nobody but a man under the influence of a woman would have taken such a course. Those were the facts I had to face, and – well, the thing came off, thanks entirely to Miss Holland. I have apologised to her twenty times already for making such a use of her, and I apologise again."

Suddenly the young German broke out.

"Ah! But were there not consolations?"

"What do you mean?"

"You and Miss Holland living by yourselves in this house – is it that you need apologise for?"

"Miss Holland never spent a single night under this roof," said Blacklock quietly.

"Not – not a night," stammered von Belke. "Then where–?"

"She stayed at a house in the neighbourhood."

The lieutenant seemed incapable of comment, and Captain Phipps observed genially.

"There seem to have been some rum goings-on behind your back, Mr Belke!"

Von Belke seemed to be realising this fact himself, and resenting it.

"You seem to have amused yourself very much by deceiving me," he remarked.

"I assure you I did nothing for fun," said Blacklock gravely, yet with a twinkle in his eye. "It was all in the way of business."

"The story that you preached, for instance!"

"Would you have felt quite happy if I had told you I had omitted to do the one thing I had professed to come here for?"

Von Belke gave a little sound that might have meant anything. Then he exclaimed–

"But your servant who was not supposed to know anything – that was to annoy me, I suppose!"

"To isolate you. I didn't want you to speak to a soul but me."

The captive sat silent for a moment, and then said "You had the house watched by the police – I see that now."

"A compliment to you, Mr Belke," smiled the Commander; and then he added, "You gave me one or two anxious moments, I may tell you. Your demand for mufti necessitated a very hurried interview with the commander of a destroyer, and old Craigie's visit very nearly upset the apple-cart. I had to tell him pretty nearly the whole truth when I got him outside. But those incidents came after the chief crisis was over. The nearest squeak was when I thought you were safely engaged with Miss Holland, and a certain officer was calling on me, who was *not* Captain Phipps. In fact, he was an even more exalted person. Miss Holland saved the situation by crying out that you were coming, or I'm afraid that would have been the end of the submarine attack."

"So?" said the young German slowly and with a very wry face, and then he turned to Eileen.

"Then, Miss Holland, every time you did me the honour to appear kind and visit me you were carrying out one of this gentleman's plans? And every word you spoke was said to entangle me in your net, or to keep me quiet while something was being done behind my back? I hope that some day you may enjoy the recollection as much as I am enjoying it now!"

"Mr Belke," she cried, "I am very deeply sorry for treating even an enemy as I treated you!"

She spoke so sincerely and with so much emotion that even Captain Phipps assumed a certain solemn expression, which was traditionally never seen on his face except when the Chaplain was actually officiating, and jumping up she came a step towards the prisoner. There she stood, a graceful and beautiful figure, her eyes glowing with fervour.

"All I can say for myself, and all I can ask you to think of when your recollections of me pain you, is only this – if you had a sister, would you have had her hesitate to do one single thing I did in order to defeat her country's enemies?"

Von Belke looked at her for a moment with frowning brow and folded arms. Then all he said was –

"Germany's cause is sacred!"

Her eyes opened very wide.

"Then what is right for Germany is wrong for her enemies?"

"Naturally. How can Germany both be right – as she is, and yet be wrong?"

"I – I don't think you quite understand what I mean," she said with a puzzled look.

"Germany never will," said Blacklock quietly. "That is why we are at war."

A tramp of footsteps sounded on the gravel outside, and Captain Phipps sprang up.

"Your guard has come for you, Mr Belke," he said. "I'm sorry to interrupt this conversation, but I'm afraid you must be moving."

III. – THE EMPTY ENVELOPE.

COMMANDER BLACKLOCK closed the front door. "Chilly night," he observed.

"It is rather," said Eileen.

The wind droned through a distant keyhole mournfully and continuously. That melancholy piping sound never rose and never fell; monotonous and unvarying it piped on and on. Otherwise the house had that peculiar feeling of quiet which houses have when stirring events are over and people have departed.

The two remaining inhabitants re-entered the parlour, glanced at one another with a half smile, and then seemed simultaneously to find a little difficulty in knowing what to do next.

"Well," said Blacklock, "our business seems over."

He felt he had spoken a little more abruptly than he intended, and would have liked to repeat his observations in a more genial tone.

"Yes," said she almost as casually, "there is nothing more to be done to-night, I suppose."

"I shall have to write up my report of our friend Mr Belke's life and last words," said he with a half laugh.

"And I have got to get over to Mrs Brown's," she replied, "and so I had better go at once."

"Oh, there's no such desperate hurry," he said hastily; "I haven't much to write up to-night. We must have some supper first."

"Yes," she agreed, "I suppose we shall begin to feel hungry soon if we don't. I'll see about it. What would you like?"

"The cold ham and a couple of boiled eggs will suit me." She agreed again.

"That won't take long, and then you can begin your report."

Again he protested hastily.

"Oh, but there's no hurry about that, I assure you. I only wanted to save trouble."

While she was away he stood before the fire, gazing absently into space and scarcely moving a muscle. The ham and boiled eggs appeared, and a little more animation became apparent, but it was not a lively feast. She talked for a little in an ordinary, cheerful way, just as though there was no very special subject for conversation; but he seemed too absent-minded and silent to respond even to these overtures, except with a brief smile and a briefer word. They had both been quite silent for about five minutes, when he suddenly said in a constrained manner, but with quite a different intonation–

"Well, I am afraid our ways part now. What are you going to do next?"

"I've been wondering," she said; "and I think if Mrs Craigie still wants me I ought to go back to her."

"Back to the Craigies!" he exclaimed. "And become – er – a governess again?"

"It will be rather dull at first," she laughed; "but one can't have such adventures as this every day, and I really have treated the Craigies rather badly. You see you told Mr Craigie the truth about my desertion of them, and they may forgive me. If they do, and if they still need me, I feel I simply must offer my services."

"It's very good of you."

She laughed again.

"It is at least as much for my own interest as Mrs Craigie's. I have nowhere else to go to and nothing else to do."

"I wish I could offer you another job like this," said he. A sparkle leapt into her eyes.

"If you ever do see any chance of making any sort of use of me – I mean of letting me be useful – you will be sure to let me know, won't you?"

"Rather! But honestly, I'm not likely to have such a bit of luck as this again."

"What will you be doing?"

"Whatever I'm told to do; the sort of thing I was on before – odd jobs of the 'hush' type. But I wish I could think of you doing something more – well, more worthy of your gifts."

"One must take one's luck as it comes," she said with an outward air of philosophy, whatever her heart whispered.

"Exactly," he agreed with emphasis. "Still –"

He broke off, and pulled a pipe out of his pocket.

"I'll leave you to smoke," she said, "and say good-night now."

"One moment!" said he, jumping up; "there's something I feel I must say. I've been rather contrite about it. I'm afraid I haven't quite played cricket so far as you are concerned. "

She looked at him quickly.

"What do you mean?" she asked.

"It's about Belke. I'm afraid Phipps was quite right in saying I'm rather cold-blooded when I am keen over a job. Perhaps it becomes a little too much of a mere problem. Getting you to treat Belke as you did, for instance. You were very nice to him to-night – though he was too German to understand how you felt – and it struck me that very possibly you had been seeing a great deal of him, and he's a nice-looking fellow, with a lot of good stuff in him, a brave man, no doubt about it, and – well, perhaps you liked him enough to make you wish I hadn't let you in for such a job. I just wondered."

She looked at him for an instant with an expression he did not quite understand; then she looked away and seemed for a moment a little embarrassed, and then she looked at him again, and he thought he had never seen franker eyes.

"You're as kind and considerate as – as, well, as you're clever!" she said with a half laugh. "But, if you only knew, if you only even had the least guess how I've longed to do something for my country – something really useful, I mean; how unutterably wretched I felt when the trifling work I was doing was stopped by a miserable neglected cold and I had to have a change, and as I'd no money I had to take this stupid job of teaching; and how I envied the women who were more fortunate and really *were* doing useful things; oh, then you'd know how grateful I feel to you! If I could make every officer in the German navy – and the army too – fall in love with me, and then hand them over to you, I'd do it fifty times over! Don't, please, talk nonsense, or think nonsense! Good-night, Mr Tiel, and perhaps its good-bye."

She laughed as she gave him his *nom-de-guerre*, and held out her hand as frankly as she had spoken. He did not take it, however.

"I'm going to escort you over to Mrs Brown's," he said with a very different expression now in his eyes.

"It's very good of you," she said; "you are sure you have time?"

"Loads!" he assured her.

He opened the door for her, but she stopped on the threshold. A young woman was waiting in the hall.

"Mrs Brown has sent her girl to escort me," she said, "so we'll have to " – she corrected herself – "we must say good-night now. Is it good-bye, or shall I see you in the morning?"

His face had become very long again.

"I'm very much afraid not. I've got to report myself with the lark. Good-bye."

The front door closed behind her, and Commander Blacklock strode back to the fire and gazed at it for some moments.

"Well," he said to himself, " I suppose, looking at things as they ought to be looked at, Mrs Brown's girl has saved me from making a damned fool of myself! Now to work: that's my proper stunt."

He threw some sheets of foolscap on the table, took out his pen, and sat down to his work. For about five minutes he stared at the foolscap, but the pen never made a movement. Then abruptly he jumped up and exclaimed–

"Dash it, I must!"

Snatching up an envelope, he thrust it in his pocket, and a moment later was out of the house.

* *

Miss Holland and her escort were about fifty yards from Mrs Brown's house when the girl started and looked back.

"There's someone crying on you!" she exclaimed.

Eileen stopped and peered back into the night. It had clouded over and was very dark. Very vaguely something seemed to loom up in the path behind them.

"Miss Holland!" cried a voice.

"It's the minister!" said the girl.

"The – who?" exclaimed Eileen; and added hastily, "Oh yes, I know who you mean."

A tall figure disengaged itself from the surrounding night.

"Sorry to trouble you," said the voice in curiously quick and jerky accents, "but I've got a note I want this girl to deliver immediately."

He handed her an envelope.

"Hand that in at the first farm on the other side of the Manse," he commanded, pointing backwards into the darkness. "I'll escort Miss Holland."

"Which hoose –" began the girl.

"The first you come to!" said the Commander peremptorily. "Quick as you can!"

Then he looked at Eileen, and for a moment said nothing.

"What's the matter?" she asked anxiously. "Has anything gone wrong?"

"Yes," he said with a half laugh, "I have. I even forgot to lick down that envelope. How the deuce I'm to explain an empty, unaddressed, unfastened envelope the Lord only knows!" His manner suddenly changed and he asked abruptly, "Are you in a desperate hurry to get in? I've something to say to you."

He paused and looked at her, but she said not a word in reply, not even to inquire what it was. A little jerkily he proceeded –

"I'm probably making just as great a fool of myself as Belke. But I couldn't let you go without asking – well, whether I am merely making a fool of myself. If you know what I mean and think I am, well, please just tell me you can manage to see yourself safely home – I know it's only about fifty yards – and I'll go and get that wretched envelope back from the girl and tell her another lie."

"Why should I think you are making a fool of yourself?" she asked in a voice that was very quiet, but not quite as even as she meant.

"Let's turn back a little way," he suggested quickly.

She said nothing, but she turned.

"Take my arm, won't you?" he suggested.

In the bitterness of his heart he was conscious that he had rapped out this proposal in his sharpest quarter-deck manner. And he had meant to speak so gently! Yet she took his arm, a little timidly it is true, but no wonder, thought he.

For a few moments they walked in silence, falling slower and slower with each step; and then they stopped. At that, speech seemed to be jerked out of him at last.

"I wonder if it's conceivable that you'd ever look upon me as anything but a calculating machine?" he inquired.

"I never thought of you in the least as that!" she exclaimed.

The gallant Commander evidently regarded this as a charitable exaggeration. He shook his head.

"You must sometimes. I know I must have seemed that sort of person."

"Not to me," she said.

He seemed encouraged, but still a little incredulous.

"Then did you ever really think of me as a human being as a – as a – " he hesitated painfully– "as a friend?"

"Yes," she said, "of course I did – always as a friend."

"Could you possibly – conceivably – think of me as" – he hesitated, and then blurted out – "as, dash it all, head over ears in love with you?"

And then suddenly the Commander realised that he had not made a fool of himself after all.

The empty envelope was duly delivered, but no explanation was required. Mrs Brown's girl supplied all the information necessary.

"Of course I knew fine what he was after," said she.

BIBLIOGRAPHY OF CLOUSTON'S WORKS

Works of Fiction - Novels

Vandrad The Viking (T. Nelson & Sons London)	1898
The Lunatic At Large (W. Blackwood and Sons)	1899
The Duke (Edward Arnold, London)	1900
The Adventures of M. D'Haricot (W. Blackwood and Sons)	1902
Our Lady's Inn (W. Blackwood & Sons)	1903
Garmiscath (W. Blackwood & Sons)	1904
Count Bunker (W. Blackwood and Sons)	1906
A County Family (John Murray, London)	1908
The Prodigal Father (Mills & Boon, London)	1909
Tales of King Fido (Mills & Boon, London)	1909
The Peer's Progress (John Murray, London)	1910
His First Offence (Mills & Boon, London)	1912
Two's Two (W. Blackwood & Sons)	1916
The Spy In Black (W. Blackwood and Sons)	1917
The Man From the Clouds (W. Blackwood & Sons)	1918
Simon (W. Blackwood & Sons)	1919
Carrington's Cases (W. Blackwood and Sons)	1920
Lunatic At Large Again (E. Nash & Grayson, London)	1922
The Lunatic Still At Large (E. Nash & Grayson, London)	1923
The Two Strange Men (E. Nash & Grayson, London)	1924
The Lunatic In Charge (John Lane, London)	1926
M Essington In Love (John Lane, London)	1927
The Jade's Progress (John Lane, London)	1928
After The Deed (W. Blackwood and Sons)	1929
Colonel Dam (W. Blackwood and Sons)	1930
The Virtuous Vamp (W. Blackwood & Sons)	1931
The Best Story Ever (W. Blackwood and Sons)	1932
Button Brains (Herbert Jenkins, London)	1933
The Chemical Baby (Herbert Jenkins, London)	1934
Real Champagne (Brown, Son & Ferguson)	1934
Our Member Mr Muttlebury (Herbert Jenkins, London)	1935
Scotland Expects (Herbert Jenkins, London)	1936
Scots Wha Ha'e (Herbert Jenkins, London)	1936
Not Since Genesis (Jarrolds, London)	1938
The Man In Steel (Jarrolds, London)	1939
Beastmark The Spy (W. Blackwood and Sons)	1941

Historical Works and Documents
(courtesy Dr Sarah Jane Gibbon)

'The Odal Families of Orkney', Old Lore Miscellany, I, 1908, 27-32.

'A Note on an Odal Family', Old Lore Miscellany, I, 1908, 135-36.

'Townships & Surnames', Old Lore Miscellany, II, 1909, 34-37.

'The Battle of Summerdale', Old Lore Miscellany, II, 1909, 95-100.

'The Odal Families of Orkney, II', Old Lore Miscellany, II, 1909, 155-162.

'The Odal Families of Orkney, III', Old Lore Miscellany, II, 1909, 227-234.

'Orkney Surnames', Old Lore Miscellany, V, 1912, 28-33.

'Orkney Surnames, II', Old Lore Miscellany, V, 1912, 63-67.

Records of the Earldom of Orkney. Edinburgh University Press, 1914.

'The Lawrikmen of Orkney', Scottish Historical Review, XIV, 1916, 49-59.

'The Old Chapels of Orkney I', Scottish Historical Review, XV, 1917, 89-105.

'The Old Chapels of Orkney II', Scottish Historical Review, XV, 1917, 223-240.

'Some Early Orkney Armorials', Proceedings of the Society of Antiquaries of Scotland, LII, 1918, 182-203.

'Two Features of the Orkney Earldom', Scottish Historical Review, XVI, 1918, 15-28.

'Some Further Early Orkney Armorials', Proceedings of the Society of Antiquaries of Scotland, LIII, 1919, 180-195.

'The Orkney Townships', Scottish Historical Review, XVII, 1919, 16-45.

'The Orkney Bailies & their Wattel', Proceedings of the Society of Antiquaries of Scotland, LV, 1921, 265-272.

'Early Orkney Rentals in Scots Money or Sterling?', Scottish Historical Review, XVIII, 1921.

'The Orkney Pennylands', Scottish Historical Review, XX, 1922, 19-27.

'Old Orkney Houses I', Proceedings of the Orkney Antiquarian Society, I, 1922-23, 11-20.

'Old Orkney Houses II', Proceedings of the Orkney Antiquarian Society, I, 1922-23, 39-48.

'Norse Heraldry in Orkney', Proceedings of the Society of Antiquaries of Scotland, LVII, 1923, 307-313.

'The Lawthing & Early Official of Orkney', Scottish Historical Review, XXI, 1923.

'Old Orkney Houses III', Proceedings of the Orkney Antiquarian Society, II, 1923-24, 7-14.

'The People & Surnames of Orkney', Proceedings of the Orkney Antiquarian Society, II, 1923-24, 31-36.

'The Orkney Lands', Proceedings of the Orkney Antiquarian Society, II, 1923-24, 61-68.

'The Goodmen & Hirdmen of Orkney', Proceedings of the Orkney Antiquarian Society, III, 1924-25, 9-19.

'The Old Orkney Mills I', Proceedings of the Orkney Antiquarian Society, III, 1924-25, 49-54.

'The Old Orkney Mills II', Proceedings of the Orkney Antiquarian Society, III, 1924-25, 65-71.

'Tradition & Fact', Proceedings of the Orkney Antiquarian Society, IV, 1925-26, 9-14.

'The Old Prebends of Orkney', Proceedings of the Orkney Antiquarian Society, IV, 1925-26, 31-36.

'An Early Orkney Castle', Proceedings of the Society of Antiquaries of Scotland, LX, 1926, 281-300.

'An Old Kirkwall House', Proceedings of the Orkney Antiquarian Society, V, 1926-27, 9-14.

'The Orkney "Bus"', Proceedings of the Orkney Antiquarian Society, V, 1926-27, 41-49.

The Orkney Parishes. 1927. Kirkwall.

'The Runrig System in Orkney', Orkney Agricultural Discussion Society Journal, II, 1927, 73-78.

'The Battle of Tankerness', Proceedings of the Orkney Antiquarian Society, VI, 1927-28, 21-25.

'Some Orkney Heraldic Rubbings', Proceedings of the Orkney Antiquarian Society, VI, 1927-28, 43-53.

'The Evidence of Stone', Proceedings of the Orkney Antiquarian Society, VII, 1928-29, 9-16.

'Three Norse Strongholds in Orkney', Proceedings of the Orkney Antiquarian Society, VII, 1928-29, 57-74.

'Six Orkney Seals', Proceedings of the Orkney Antiquarian Society, VIII, 1929-30, 9-16.

'Three More Seals', Proceedings of the Orkney Antiquarian Society, VIII, 1929-30, 31-34.

'An Old Norse Drinking Horn', Proceedings of the Orkney Antiquarian Society, VIII, 1929-30, 57-62.

'A Fresh View of the Settlement of Orkney', Proceedings of the Orkney Antiquarian Society, IX, 1930-31, 35-40.

'The Orkney Arms', Proceedings of the Orkney Antiquarian Society, IX, 1930-31, 57-60.

Early Norse Castles. 1931. Kirkwall.

'Tammaskirk in Rendall', Proceedings of the Orkney Antiquarian Society, X, 1931-32, 9-16.

'Our Ward Hills & Ensigns', Proceedings of the Orkney Antiquarian Society, X, 1931-32, 33-42.

A History of Orkney. 1932. Kirkwall.

'Something about Maeshowe', Proceedings of the Orkney Antiquarian Society, XI, 1932-33, 9-18.

'The Origin of the Halcros', Proceedings of the Orkney Antiquarian Society, XI, 1932-33, 59-66.

'The Origin of the Orkney Chiefs', Proceedings of the Orkney Antiquarian Society, XII, 1933-34, 29-40.

'The Aikerness Stone', Proceedings of the Orkney Antiquarian Society, XIV, 1936-37, 9-20.

'Orkney & the Hudson's Bay Company', The Beaver, Dec. 1936, March & September 1937.

'The Armorial de Berry', Proceedings of the Society of Antiquaries of Scotland, LXXII, 1937-38, 84-114.

'Orkney & the Archer Guards', Proceedings of the Orkney Antiquarian Society, XV, 1937-39, 15-32.

'Orkney & the Archer Guards - a further note', Proceedings of the Orkney Antiquarian Society, XV, 1937-39, 33-34.

'James Sinclair of Brecks', Proceedings of the Orkney Antiquarian Society, XV, 1937-39, 61-68.

The Family of Clouston, 1948 & 2004. Kirkwall.

CITY AND ROYAL BURGH OF KIRKWALL

WARNING

The Provost, Magistrates, and Councillors of Kirkwall hereby recommend the inhabitants to vacate their homes and proceed to the country, without any delay, should the town be Bombarded by the enemy.

W. J. HEDDLE,
TOWN CLERK.

KIRKWALL, 26th April 1918.

Printed at the "Orkney Herald" Office, Kirkwall.

Above: A warning poster.
Below: Searchlight post on Flotta

Above: Men from the Ness Battery, near Stromness
Below: The seaplane station at Scapa Bay near Kirkwall

Above: "Action Somewhere Not In France". This photo was taken at the Hoxa Battery, South Ronaldsay. The title was to prevent the location from being identified.
Below: One of the Hoxa searchlight posts at the entrance to Scapa Flow.

Above: The SS St Ola although not featured in the book, had an important role in the 1939 film of
THE SPY IN BLACK, playing the part of the St Magnus. She sailed between Stromness and Scrabster
from1892 until 1951 and was the longest serving ferry on that route.
Below: Part of the British Fleet at anchor in Scapa Flow prior to the First World War.

Above: Squadron Commander Dunning landing his Sopwith Pup on HMS Furious on 5th August 1917, the world's first landing of an aircraft onto a moving ship. Sadly Dunning was killed days later when attempting his third landing.

Below: HMS Vanguard in Scapa Flow. On 9th July 1917 she blew up at anchor off the island of Flotta with the loss of around one thousand men. As this incident was the result of an accident rather than from enemy fire, it was many years before the wreck was designated as a war grave.

Above: A group of servicemen at Kings Hard, Flotta

Below: Breckan Gun Battery, Holm overlooking Kirk Sound in the days before the Churchill Barriers were built. Note the blockships that had been used to prevent enemy ships entering Scapa Flow.

Above: View from the hill above Houton overlooking the seaplane station. In the background are some of the ships of the German Fleet at anchor at the end of the war. On 21st June 1919 the fleet scuttled itself.

Below: J Storer Clouston in his study

A Clouston family photograph at Smoogro, Orphir. As well as the author, the picture features his wife, children and parents.

THE SPY IN BLACK – THE RIGHT ROAD?

Sandra Miller and Elaine Clarke

ONE OF THE nice things about reading a book based in the area where you live is trying to identify the locations and places the writer describes. *The Spy in Black* is a work of fiction, but the author J Storer Clouston appears to have used real locations. Trying to identify these locations has been a challenge, with the ever changing Orkney coastline and sadly the author no longer with us to confirm or deny that he had specific locations and directions in mind.

When the idea came that an attempt should be made to try and establish the route Lieutenant Belke took around Orkney it seemed a fairly daunting task as nowhere in the book is anywhere named but as they say the clues were there. Where some parts are quite obviously specific locations and were fairly easily recognisable other parts have perhaps been subject to the author's imagination. Certainly the distances involved in some places were much closer than presented in the book and some much further apart.

As far as can be established Belke landed in Birsay Bay. When trying to find this location there was much debate as to whether this was here, Skaill or Marwick, the final decision for this location was made once the rest of the route was roughly established. He pushes what he describes as his bicycle across the grass towards a rough road which then connected with what he describes as the highroad.

Once on the road he sees a loch on his left – Boardhouse, then encounters what is described as an eerie looking standing stone - Quoybune. Making good time he heads along the side of the loch only to break down and to have to retrace his steps to where he started but this time heads up hill towards Marwick where he finds a ruined cottage to shelter in

and repair his motorbike.

The next morning having been surprised by the arrival of an old woman he heads back the way he came. Round by the loch and standing stone this time travelling further along the road than before turning onto a side road that leads to the coast, this turning is at what is now the Twatt Kirk and going through what he describes as a marshy valley (The Loons) to reach the junction where he looks over to Marwick Bay.

Turning left he heads towards Skaill Bay describing his wide view over inland country. He descends towards Skaill Bay where he hides behind a wall between the road and the sea, where he believes he cannot be seen, however he is discovered.

He feels he has aroused suspicion and quickly makes his way along the road at the side of Skaill Loch, concerned he may be being followed he scatters tacks on the road to slow down his pursuers.

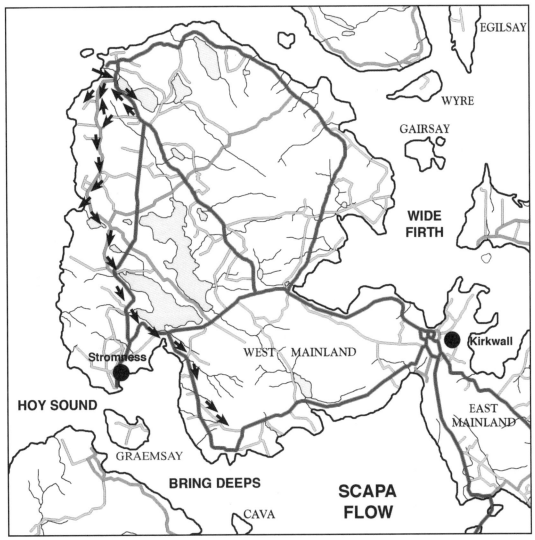

The route taken by Lieutenant Belke with his motorcycle

The final part of the route does not sit so obviously in the mind's eye as he travels towards the Brig of Waithe where he describes his first view of Scapa Flow and the Hoy hills beyond it. Following along the road to Orphir he ascends the hill to the top of Scorradale and there gets his first proper view of the fleet at harbour in the Flow.

Hiding in hollows in the heather he describes watching the manse. Scorradale House and its prominent location fits the description of the house in the book where the story unfolds.

Sandra Miller and Elaine Clarke were appointed as the first ever Orkney Rangers with specific responsibility for Orkney's World Heritage sites; the posts are funded by Scottish Natural Heritage and Historic Scotland. Their brief is to facilitate the interpretation of the World Heritage sites for the benefit of local people and visitors. They show the history and ecology of these sensitive areas through lectures, guided walks, workshops and by working with educational groups.